Nothing But

The Truth

By David Muncaster

Nothing But The Truth

Stephen Bellamy and Susan Ives stand accused of murdering Stephen's wife, Lola. According to the prosecution, Susan found that her husband was having an affair with Lola, and she persuaded Stephen to help her put a stop to it. With a knife. But, as the witnesses are called to give their evidence, it becomes clear that things are much more complicated than they first appear. Assuming, of course, that everyone is telling nothing but the truth.

This play for six actors is inspired by the Bellamy trial from over 100 years ago but has been updated and set in Northwest England in the present day. Four actors play the Judge, the Usher, the Prosecution, and the Defence. The other two actors play everyone else, including all the witnesses and the accused.

The audience is invited to select a jury and decide whether the defendants are guilty or not guilty before the truth is finally revealed.

The main characters and their relationships

Before Patrick went to University

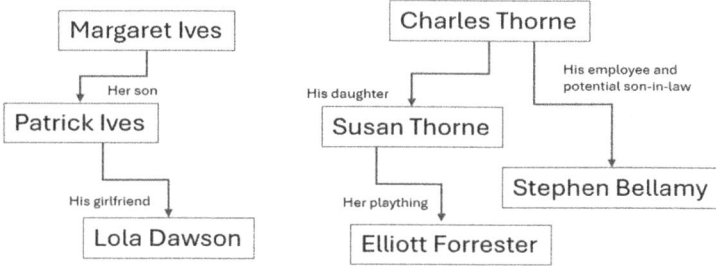

Margaret Ives		Charles Thorne	
Her son ↓		His daughter ↓	His employee and potential son-in-law
Patrick Ives		Susan Thorne	
His girlfriend ↓		Her plaything ↓	Stephen Bellamy
Lola Dawson		Elliott Forrester	

While Patrick was at University

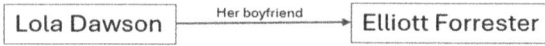

Lola Dawson	— Her boyfriend →	Elliott Forrester

After Patrick returned from University

Patrick Ives	Move to London →	Susan Thorne
Margaret Ives		Becomes Susan Ives

Title: Nothing But The Truth
Author: David Muncaster
Copyright Year: 2024
ISBN: 978-1-4452-2677-4
Imprint: Lulu.com

9 781445 226774

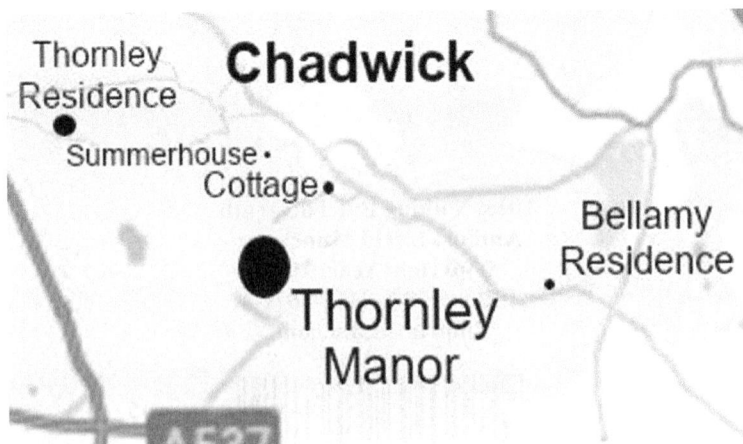

Nothing But The Truth

Characters:

Actor 1 (M/F)	**Usher**
Actor 2 (M/F)	**Judge**
Actor 3 (M/F)	**Defence**
Actor 4 (M/F)	**Prosecution**
Actor 5 (M)	**Stephen Bellamy** – Accused of murdering Lola
	Dr Brock - Pathologist
	David Thorne – Brother of Susan Ives
	Elliot Forrester – Former lover of Lola
	Paul Harrison – Friend of Elliot and Patrick
	Darren York - Handyman
	Sergeant Calvert – First police officer on scene
	Patrick Ives – Husband of Susan
	Tom Williams – Wild camper
Actor 6 (F)	**Susan Ives** – Accused of murdering Lola
	Chloe Langton – Estate Agent
	Kathleen Page - Nanny
	Fiona Biggs – Childhood friend of Lola
	Margaret Ives – Mother of Patrick
	Melanie Cooper – Housekeeper
	Laura Roberts – Friend of Margaret
	Joanne Trimble – Bus Driver
	Dr Gabriel – DNA expert

ACT ONE

A courtroom with a witness stand, a bench for the judge, and tables for the barristers. The judge and barristers may have laptops. If separate actors play the defendants, then there is a dock; otherwise, the actors playing multiple roles sit to the side when not on stage. Twelve chairs are arranged for the jury, who are selected from the audience. They should be visible to the remainder of the audience but not in the direct line of sight.

USHER: Court rise. (*All rise, and the JUDGE enters.*)

JUDGE: Please be seated. (*All sit*). Crown versus Stephen Bellamy and Susan Ives.

DEFENCE: Your honour.

PROSECUTION: Your honour.

JUDGE: Ladies and gentlemen, you are the jurors who will try this case. At its close, you will retire and vote upon your verdict. I instruct you to listen to the testimony carefully and pronounce your judgement to the best of your ability and integrity. You will not discuss this case with anyone outside of this courtroom, and your deliberations will all be held in private until you determine whether each of the defendants is guilty or not guilty. Their fate rests in your hands. We will start with the case for the prosecution.

PROSECUTION: Thank you, your honour. Ladies and gentlemen of the jury, on the night of the nineteenth of June last year, a singularly cruel and ruthless murder took place. On that summer night, a young woman came to meet her lover. She, another man's wife; he, another woman's husband, but love made her hasten her step as she made her way to an unoccupied Gatekeeper's Cottage on the edge of her village. But it was not love that was waiting for her in the cottage.

The following morning, Chloe Langton of Langton and Lloyd Estate Agents arrived at the cottage with a prospective buyer and was surprised to find the front door unlocked. To her horror, she discovered the body of Lola Bellamy in the sitting room, her white dress covered in blood; there were signs of a struggle, and a heavy brass table lamp lay on the floor. She had clearly been stabbed several times, and it was later discovered that a necklace and several rings that Lola had been wearing were now missing.

The man on trial is Stephen Bellamy, the husband of Lola. The woman who sits beside him is Susan Ives. She is the wife of Patrick Ives, who was Lola's lover and the man that Lola was going to meet that night. Murder is an ugly and repellent thing, but this murder, I think that you will agree, is an especially ugly and repellent one. These two supposedly respectable and decent citizens were, with Lola's blood still on their hands, cool, collected, and calm enough to remove her jewellery in order to make this murder look like a robbery gone wrong.

I think it will be useful for you to know something of the background, and I will try to present this to you as succinctly as possible. Cheshire is a beautiful county containing many lovely homes and pleasant communities. Not far from the upmarket town of Alderley Edge lies the flourishing village of Chadwick, which boasts two of the best gastropubs in the area, a post office, and a delightful cricket club. On the edge of the village lies the estate of Patrick Ives and his wife. This former farmhouse has been extensively remodelled, and the grounds now boast a walled garden, tennis courts, and a new structure containing a heated swimming pool with a jacuzzi, sauna, and private fitness suite. Patrick Ives is a thirty-two-year-old man who has a surprisingly successful career as an investment banker. I use the word surprisingly advisedly because the community was greatly surprised when, around seven years ago, Patrick married Susan Thorne and set about building a career, having never previously shown much inclination to be what we might call a high-flyer.

At the time of the murder, Mr. Ives's household consisted of his wife, his two children, his mother, a friend of hers staying for a few weeks, and a live-in nanny. For the time being, the only member who concerns us is his wife, Susan Ives. She is the daughter of the very wealthy Charles Thorne and grew up on the Thorne estate near the village. Her mother died shortly after Susan was born, but she was idolised by both her father and her older brother. As childhood gave way to teenage years, she showed little interest in entering into a relationship, so it came as a surprise when, seven years ago, she took off to London with Patrick Ives when he returned from university. Her father felt Patrick was unsuitable and begged her to stay in Chadwick, but she did not listen. Infuriated, he cut her out of his will, but, as it happens, he died penniless when his business failed just two years later.

Shortly after her father's death, Susan returned from London, married to Patrick and with two young children. Accompanying them was Patrick's mother, Margaret. Patrick had got a job in investment banking, and his rise had been meteoric. Just three years after leaving Chadwick, they returned, purchased the old farmhouse, and refurbished it to the very highest standard. On the surface, they seemed happy. They had a lovely home, two lovely children, and Patrick was earning far more than they could possibly spend.

About a mile from the Ives's beautiful estate lies another farmhouse. This has not been refurbished; there is no tennis court or private fitness suite. Behind a rickety fence lies a shabby cottage and dilapidated garage. This is the home of Charlotte Bellamy, known to everyone as Lola. As a child, Lola Dawson grew up in a comfortable, unpretentious house just off Chadwick High Street next door to a house that had been divided into flats. Here lived the aforementioned Margaret Ives and her son, Patrick. Mrs. Ives had lived in the village for a number of years and gained a good reputation, and some income, as a piano teacher. She also earned money through a bit of childminding and dog walking, often accompanied by the devoted Patrick.

Having been neighbours for a number of years, when they were both around seventeen, Lola and Patrick became boyfriend and girlfriend. They appeared to have completely fallen in love and did everything together. When Patrick left to go to university in Newcastle, their friends assumed that he and Lola would live together when he returned. But they didn't take into account how lonely Lola would become when Patrick was away.

To counter that loneliness, let me introduce to the story one Elliot Forrester. Elliot was a handsome, practical, and popular lad. He had his own car and would happily be the designated driver when the young people of Chadwick sought entertainment beyond the boundaries of the village. Lola fell in with this crowd and allowed herself to be whisked off to gigs in Manchester, shopping trips in Wilmslow, or days out in the Peak District, but whoever was in the party, it always seemed to be Lola who was the last one to be dropped off after every outing. Three weeks before Patrick was due to complete his studies and return to Chadwick from university, Mr. and Mrs. Dawson sent out cards inviting guests to a celebration of the engagement of their daughter Charlotte to Elliot Forrester. This came as a surprise to many of the residents of Chadwick, none more so than the defendant Susan Thorne, who had known Elliot for a number of years and, despite her apparent indifference to him, imagined that he would be available whenever she wanted.

Patrick Ives, however, did not appear to be too perturbed to find Lola in the arms of another, and, before very long, he and Susan Thorne became inseparable despite the very obvious displeasure of Susan's father. Charles Thorne favoured Stephen Bellamy as his future son-in-law. A successful partner in Charles's firm, Stephen was considered a "catch" due to his good looks, intelligence, and business acumen. But Stephen had no interest in Susan and soon became infatuated himself with Lola. In the space of one week, three significant events took place in the lives of those I have discussed. On the Monday, after a very public shouting match with Elliot, Lola broke off her engagement to him. On the Wednesday, Patrick Ives and Susan Thorne left for London without a word to anyone, and then, on the Friday, Lola Dawson and Stephen Bellamy announced that they were getting married.

Seven years have now passed since that momentous week, and the seeds of discord, heartbreak, envy, and malice planted back then have now grown to become a mighty vine heavy with bitter fruit, ripe for harvest. But on a pleasant summer's day in June last year, Chadwick Cricket Green seemed a most tranquil place. It is late afternoon, and the people I have introduced to you are gathered there in a scene that could not be more English. Lola Bellamy is there waiting for her husband to return from the field. Susan Ives is there despite her husband being away in Manchester on business. Instead, she has Elliot Forrester for company, and the pair are in deep conversation a little away from the others. You may ask yourself how it is possible that events can have taken such a horrific turn just a few hours later. You may ask yourself how it is possible that Susan Ives, a seemingly respectable and intelligent young woman, can have wilfully, brutally, and deliberately murdered another woman. How is it possible that the charismatic Stephen Bellamy can have aided and abetted her in this act?

We know that Susan's comfortable existence was severely threatened by Patrick's affair, and the hatred of the woman responsible has led her to this desperate crime. As for Stephen Bellamy, his love for Lola was the only light in his drab and colourless life. We can only imagine the pain he felt on learning that his wife was being unfaithful.

I will prove that it is not only possible that the defendants committed this heinous crime but that it is certain beyond any reasonable doubt. I will call my first witness, Chloe Langton.

CHLOE LANGTON is led to the witness box and given a Bible and a card with the wording of the oath.

CHLOE: I swear by Almighty God that the evidence I shall give shall be the truth, the whole truth, and nothing but the truth.

PROSECUTION: Would you please state your profession?

CHLOE: I am an estate agent.

PROSECUTION: Your office is in Chadwick?

CHLOE: No, Wilmslow.

PROSECUTION: But you are offering for sale Orchard House, Chadwick?

CHLOE: That is correct.

PROSECUTION: Who is the current owner?

CHLOE: It was left by Charles Thorne to his son, David.

PROSECUTION: Who has listed it with you to sell?

CHLOE: Sell or rent. Preferably sell.

PROSECUTION: Has there been much interest?

CHLOE: Limited. It is a large property, too large for most, and in need of modernisation, but a client visiting the area noticed it in our window and requested a viewing before he returned to Scotland.

PROSECUTION: When was this?

CHLOE: He came into the office on Saturday morning, June the nineteenth last year. The viewing was the following morning.

PROSECUTION: Could you describe what happened when you took your client to the viewing?

CHLOE: Yes. We pulled up at the Gatekeeper's Cottage to collect the key to Orchard House. I only held a key to the cottage. I noticed that the front door was slightly ajar and was concerned that there might have been a break-in. I went into the hallway and found the door to the dining room on the left closed, but the door to the living room was open. I could only see a small section of the room until I stepped inside.

PROSECUTION: Was your client with you?

CHLOE: A little behind me.

PROSECUTION: Go on.

CHLOE: I saw the body of a young woman in a white dress on the floor next to an overturned side table and a smashed lamp.

PROSECUTION: Was her head facing you or her feet?

CHLOE: Her feet. Her head was on the fireplace.

PROSECUTION: Did you notice anything else?

CHLOE: Yes. There was a great deal of blood.

PROSECUTION: Where?

CHLOE: Mainly on her dress, but there was also some on the carpet.

PROSECUTION: Could you describe the dress?

CHLOE: It was soaked in blood.

PROSECUTION: Yes, but what sort of dress was it? Casual? Ball gown?

CHLOE: Well, quite smart but not formal. It was sleeveless.

PROSECUTION: What did you do next?

CHLOE: I said to my client…

PROSECUTION: Not what you said; what did you do?

CHLOE: I called 999, of course.

PROSECUTION: Which service did you request?

CHLOE: Police.

PROSECUTION: Not an ambulance?

CHLOE: There didn't seem much point.

PROSECUTION: And what did you tell the police?

CHLOE: That I had discovered the body of Lola Bellamy.

PROSECUTION: You recognised her?

CHLOE: Yes, she was a friend of my sister-in-law. We'd met a few times.

PROSECUTION: I'm sorry; it must have been a great shock. Did you call anyone else?

CHLOE: Yes. I called David Thorne as a courtesy.

PROSECUTION: Why was the key to the main house kept in the Gatekeeper's Cottage? Wouldn't it be easier for you to have a copy in the office?

CHLOE: There was such little interest it didn't seem worthwhile, but we thought we might have more luck with the cottage on its own.

PROSECUTION: But wouldn't it be safer if you held both keys? Anyone breaking into the cottage would then have access to the main house.

CHLOE: Oh, the key to the main house wasn't usually kept in the cottage. David dropped it off the previous evening. I'd called to say we had a viewing.

PROSECUTION: I see. What time did David Thorne drop off the key?

CHLOE: I have no idea, but it couldn't have been before seven in the evening. I'd been trying to contact him all day and finally got through at 6.30pm. He had apparently left his phone at home by accident.

PROSECUTION: Does he live in Chadwick?

CHLOE: No, Knutsford. That's why I said seven. It would take thirty minutes to drive to the cottage.

PROSECUTION: Thank you. No further questions.

JUDGE: Anything from the defence?

DEFENCE: Just a couple of questions. Was it entirely David Thorne's suggestion to drop off the key at the cottage?

CHLOE: Yes.

DEFENCE: And you have no idea what time that was. It could have been 7pm or it could have been midnight.

CHLOE: That is correct.

DEFENCE: Thank you. That is all.

PROSECUTION: Can we have Dr. Brock, please?

CHLOE exits, and DR. BROCK enters the witness box and takes the oath.

DR. BROCK: I swear by Almighty God that the evidence I shall give will be the truth, the whole truth, and nothing but the truth.

PROSECUTION: Dr. Brock, what is your profession?

DR. BROCK: I am a forensic pathologist.

PROSECUTION: You perform autopsies?

DR. BROCK: That is correct.

PROSECUTION: And you performed the autopsy on Lola Bellamy?

DR. BROCK: Yes.

PROSECUTION: Where did you first see her body?

DR. BROCK: I was called to the crime scene.

PROSECUTION: Was the body in the position described by Chloe Langton?

DR. BROCK: It was.

PROSECUTION: The police are not permitted to move the body until death is confirmed.

DR. BROCK: That is correct.

PROSECUTION: Was the body then taken to the mortuary?

DR. BROCK: Not straight away. They moved it into the other downstairs room so that they could conduct a proper search of the crime scene without having to wait for the ambulance before they could start.

PROSECUTION: Were you able to establish a cause of death?

DR. BROCK: Yes. There was a single puncture wound to the heart caused by a bladed instrument, such as a kitchen knife. This passed between the ribs to a depth of around seven centimetres.

PROSECUTION: Would it have required a degree of force to push the knife in that far?

DR. BROCK: No. Had it struck a rib, it would have required some strength to deflect it, but it was a clean wound that could have been inflicted by most adults. Or a strong child, even. I should say that the cause of death was a single puncture wound, but there were other nonfatal wounds in the same area.

PROSECUTION: How many?

DR. BROCK: Five in total.

PROSECUTION: Would death have been instantaneous?

DR. BROCK: No, but it would have been quick. A few minutes, maybe.

PROSECUTION: So, Lola will have suffered. Might she have called out?

DR. BROCK: I really cannot say.

PROSECUTION shows Dr. Brock a photograph.

PROSECUTION: Could this have been the knife used?

DR. BROCK: It is possible.

PROSECUTION: Please describe it to the jury.

DR. BROCK: It looks like it is a jackknife with a black handle.

PROSECUTION: Is there anything else in the photograph?

DR. BROCK: There is a tape measure that indicates the blade to be around ten centimetres.

PROSECUTION: Enough to have done the job.

DR. BROCK: Absolutely.

PROSECUTION: Thank you, Dr. Brock.

PROSECUTION sits. DEFENCE stands.

DEFENCE: No questions.

PROSECUTION: I call my next witness, Kathleen Page.

DR. BROCK exits, and KATHLEEN enters the witness box and takes the oath.

KATHLEEN: I do solemnly, sincerely, and truly declare and affirm that the evidence I shall give shall be the truth, the whole truth, and nothing but the truth.

PROSECUTION: Please state your name.

KATHLEEN: Kathleen Page.

PROSECUTION: Ms. Page, were you employed as a nanny by Susan Ives on the 19th of June last year?

KATHLEEN: Yes.

PROSECUTION: And can you tell us when you left her employment?

KATHLEEN: The twenty-first.

PROSECUTION: Please tell us what you were doing at eight o'clock the evening of the nineteenth.

KATHLEEN: Yes. There was nothing worth watching on TV, so I decided to read. I then remembered that I'd left my book on the bench at the bottom of the garden, so I went to fetch it.

PROSECUTION: Are you sure of the time?

KATHLEEN: Yes.

PROSECUTION: How?

KATHLEEN: I'd just been looking at the TV guide on my phone.

PROSECUTION: Did you see anyone before you left the house?

KATHLEEN: Yes. Patrick, Mr. Ives. He was just coming out of the living room.

PROSECUTION: Did you speak to him?

KATHLEEN: Yes. He asked me if the children were still up. I said they were in bed but probably still awake.

PROSECUTION: Did Mr. Ives love his children?

KATHLEEN: Oh yes, he was devoted to them.

DEFENCE: Your Honour, if I may. This is just an opinion. The witness cannot possibly know for sure.

JUDGE: I agree. Please take more care in your questioning.

PROSECUTION: I apologise, but I do have a reason for asking. I am trying to establish that Susan Ives would know that, should she and her husband divorce, Patrick would fight for custody of the children. There is no better witness to the devotion that he had for them than their nanny.

JUDGE: Very well. I shan't ask the jury to disregard the answer, but please remember that it is an opinion.

PROSECUTION: Thank you, Your Honour. And was Susan Ives as devoted as her husband?

DEFENCE: Your Honour!

JUDGE: That is enough. Please do not take liberties.

PROSECUTION: My apologies, once again. Was Susan with her husband when you saw him coming out of the living room?

KATHLEEN: No, she had already said goodnight to the children. I assumed she was still in the living room.

PROSECUTION: And did you see Patrick go into the children's bedroom?

KATHLEEN: Not exactly, but he went upstairs. I am sure that is where he was headed.

PROSECUTION: Are all the bedrooms upstairs?

KATHLEEN: The children's room and my room are on the top floor. The main bedrooms are on the first floor.

PROSECUTION: Do Mr. and Mrs. Ives have separate bedrooms?

KATHLEEN: No, they share a room, but Mrs. Ives, sorry, I refer to Patrick's mother as Mrs. Ives, Mrs. Ives's bedroom is also on the first floor.

PROSECUTION: And what about the ground floor?

KATHLEEN: There is a living room, dining room, kitchen, utility room, a second sitting room, and a study that is used as an office. I think that is all in the main building.

DEFENCE: Is all this relevant?

PROSECUTION: I intend to show that it is. Thank you for the description. Now, please go on. Did you see anyone other than Patrick Ives?

KATHLEEN: Yes, I saw Mrs. Ives, Patrick's mother. She was in the rose garden. She often stayed out there on a summer's evening.

PROSECUTION: What happened next?

KATHLEEN: I collected my book and returned to the house.

PROSECUTION: And you saw no one else?

KATHLEEN: No, but I heard Susan on the telephone as I passed the study. The window was open, you see.

PROSECUTION: You are sure it was Susan?

KATHLEEN: Yes. I had just seen Mrs. Ives outside, and anyway, I recognised the voice.

PROSECUTION: Did you hear anything of what she was saying?

KATHLEEN: Yes, she was asking to speak to Lola.

PROSECUTION: Let's just go back a bit. What exactly did you hear?

KATHLEEN: I heard Susan say, "Stephen, it's Susan. Is Lola there?"

PROSECUTION: So, there is no doubt she was speaking to Stephen Bellamy.

KATHLEEN: I'm sure of it.

PROSECUTION: But you don't know if she was asking to speak to Lola or ascertaining whether she was there or not.

KATHLEEN: Oh. Yes, I suppose you are right.

PROSECUTION: Did you hear any more?

KATHLEEN: Yes. She said, "When did she leave? Are you sure that is where she has gone?" Then she said, "Has Elliot said anything to you?" and then, "Can you come to pick me up? It's really important."

PROSECUTION: Is that it?

KATHLEEN: No. She said, "Come to the back lane. I'll meet you there in ten minutes."

PROSECUTION: You are absolutely sure that is what she said.

KATHLEEN: Yes. I remember it because I repeated it shortly afterwards.

PROSECUTION: What do you mean?

KATHLEEN: I went back up to my room, and just as I reached the second-floor landing, Patrick came out of the children's bedroom. I thought he should know what I had heard.

PROSECUTION: So, you told him?

KATHLEEN: Not straight away. Susan called up the stairs to ask him if he was going out again. He said that he was going to visit his friend, Paul, to play poker, and she said that, in that case, she'd go round to see her friend Lisa Langton. Then the front door slammed.

PROSECUTION: Then you told Patrick what you had heard?

KATHLEEN: Yes.

PROSECUTION: Word for word?

KATHLEEN: Yes. And when I had finished, he said, "Oh my God! Someone has told her."

DEFENCE: Your Honour!

JUDGE: Ms. Page, you must only answer the questions put to you.

KATHLEEN: Oh. Sorry.

PROSECUTION: I have no more questions.

JUDGE: Do you wish to cross-examine?

DEFENCE: Yes, please. Ms. Page, you seem to recall the events of that evening very well.

KATHLEEN: I have an excellent memory.

DEFENCE: Do you recall what book you were reading at the time?

KATHLEEN: Yes, I do, as it happens. It was 'Gone Girl' by Gillian Flynn.

DEFENCE: Was it your own copy?

KATHLEEN: No, it was from the study.

DEFENCE: Did Susan Ives say you could borrow it?

KATHLEEN: Well, no. I…

DEFENCE: How about Patrick? Did you ask him if you could borrow a book?

KATHLEEN: I don't think it was necessary. I don't imagine either of them would object.

DEFENCE: Did you regard yourself as a member of the family?

KATHLEEN: Not at all.

DEFENCE: Did you take your meals with them?

KATHLEEN: No.

DEFENCE: Spend your evenings with them?

KATHLEEN: No.

DEFENCE: No. You rather resented them because of that, didn't you? You spent all day looking after their children and felt they should have been more welcoming. More grateful.

PROSECUTION: Your Honour, this has nothing to do with the case.

DEFENCE: Oh, but it does. I propose to demonstrate that Ms. Page detests Susan Ives and would not hesitate to throw her under a bus.

PROSECUTION: Your Honour!

JUDGE: Let's keep things civil. You may answer the question, Ms. Page.

KATHLEEN: What was the question?

DEFENCE: Is it true that you resented being treated as a servant?

KATHLEEN: Not at all.

DEFENCE: Really?

KATHLEEN: It never entered my head.

DEFENCE: It never entered your head! No cause for complaint?

KATHLEEN: Never.

DEFENCE: You were perfectly satisfied with the situation.

KATHLEEN: Perfectly.

DEFENCE: (*Producing a note.*) Is this your handwriting?

KATHLEEN: It looks like it.

DEFENCE: I didn't ask if it looked like it; I asked if it was.

KATHLEEN: I couldn't say, for certain. It could be a forgery.

DEFENCE: Perhaps you would read it out for us and then tell us, using your excellent memory, if you recall writing it.

KATHLEEN: I… Well, um…

DEFENCE: Would you prefer me to read it out?

KATHLEEN: I recall writing it, yes.

DEFENCE: Oh, but Ms. Page. We have moved on from recollection and are now on content. Please be so kind as to read it aloud.

KATHLEEN: (*Reading*.) "I'm sorry to resort to this, but I've tried to speak to you on a number of occasions, and it is clear that you will not discuss the matter with me face to face. My understanding is that my position in this household entitles me to bed and board; however, as you do not wish me to eat with the family, it seems that my evening meal consists of leftovers barely fit for human consumption. Please let me know how you will remedy this."

DEFENCE: When did you send that?

KATHLEEN: In May last year.

DEFENCE: And how do you reconcile that with being perfectly satisfied with your situation and having no cause for complaint?

KATHLEEN: I had forgotten all about it. Anyway, Susan rectified the situation immediately.

DEFENCE: I beg your pardon!

KATHLEEN: She sorted it straight away.

DEFENCE: She sorted it! Didn't she tell you that if you were not satisfied, you could have a month's salary in lieu of notice and leave the next day?

KATHLEEN: That is not true at all.

DEFENCE: Are you saying that you didn't beg Susan to give you another chance?

KATHLEEN: Nothing of the sort. Susan was very regretful of the way I'd been treated. There was no mention of me leaving.

DEFENCE: I suppose you are going to tell me that it is also untrue that a month later, two days before the murder in fact, she gave you a month's salary in lieu of notice after you took the afternoon off work without permission.

KATHLEEN: Yes, that is also untrue.

DEFENCE: You didn't take the afternoon off work?

KATHLEEN: I did, but with Patrick's permission.

DEFENCE: Ms. Page. Do you know what perjury is?

PROSECUTION: Your Honour!

JUDGE: I see no reason why a witness should be asked to give a definition of perjury. Please ensure that your questions are pertinent to the case.

DEFENCE: Thank you, Your Honour, I will. Ms. Page, when you realised that Susan was talking on the telephone, did you stop outside the window to listen?

KATHLEEN: Yes.

DEFENCE: You were eavesdropping.

KATHLEEN: I'm only human.

DEFENCE: You heard her quite clearly?

KATHLEEN: Yes.

DEFENCE: So, anyone would have been able to hear her clearly?

KATHLEEN: Yes, if they were standing where I was.

DEFENCE: She was making a secret rendezvous, yet she was speaking loud enough for anyone passing to hear.

KATHLEEN: She probably didn't think anyone would be passing.

DEFENCE: You were not asked what Susan Ives thought; you were asked if anyone passing would hear.

KATHLEEN: Yes, they would.

DEFENCE: Could Patrick have heard it?

KATHLEEN: He was upstairs.

DEFENCE: I didn't ask where he was; I asked you if he could have heard it.

KATHLEEN: If he had been where I was standing, he would have done it.

DEFENCE: Would you mind repeating what Susan said on the telephone?

KATHLEEN: All of it?

DEFENCE: Yes, please.

KATHLEEN: "Stephen, it's Susan. Is Lola there? When did she leave? Are you sure that is where she has gone? Has Elliot said anything to you?

Can you come to pick me up? It's really important. Come to the back lane. I'll meet you there in ten minutes."

DEFENCE: That is very impressive. Word for word what you said before.

KATHLEEN: I remember it because I wrote it down.

DEFENCE: You wrote it down! When?

KATHLEEN: As I stood listening. I wrote it on a blank page at the back of Gone Girl.

DEFENCE: Why?

KATHLEEN: It sounded important. I wanted to make sure I didn't make any mistakes.

DEFENCE: Then you ran straight to Patrick Ives, bursting to tell him something that you thought would wreck his marriage.

KATHLEEN: No, I wanted to help them.

DEFENCE: Help them! How?

KATHLEEN: I thought that Patrick might nip things in the bud.

DEFENCE: Nip what in the bud?

KATHLEEN: I assumed that Susan must be having an affair with Stephen. I didn't know that Patrick was seeing Lola.

DEFENCE: I see. You were just bringing him glad tidings of his wife's infidelity. That is all, Ms. Page.

PROSECUTION: One moment. Kathleen, you said that Patrick's mother was in the rose garden. Was this visible from the study where you saw Susan?

KATHLEEN: Yes, a path leads from there down to the rose garden.

PROSECUTION: And Susan believed both you and Patrick to be up on the top floor?

KATHLEEN: Yes.

PROSECUTION: You often visit the study to borrow books. (*He shows her the photograph of the knife.*) Have you ever seen this knife before?

KATHLEEN: Yes, Patrick keeps it on the desk in the study.

PROSECUTION: And, just to be clear, Susan Ives will have passed the desk as she left the study after finishing her phone call.

KATHLEEN: That is correct.

PROSECUTION: Thank you. No further questions. Can we have David Thorne next?

KATHLEEN exits, and DAVID enters the witness box and takes the oath.

DAVID: I swear by Almighty God that the evidence I shall give shall be the truth, the whole truth, and nothing but the truth.

PROSECUTION: Mr. Thorne, please state your relationship to the defendant, Susan Ives.

DAVID: I am her brother and proud of it.

PROSECUTION: Thank you; the affection that you hold for your sister is noted. You are the sole owner of Orchard House?

DAVID: Yes, I'm afraid our father hated Patrick and left Suzie nothing in his will.

PROSECUTION: How do you feel about Patrick?

DAVID: I have been quite fond of him, but in the present circumstances, I will reserve judgement.

PROSECUTION: You are devoted to your sister, aren't you?

DAVID: I'd do anything for her.

PROSECUTION: Turning to the matter at hand. Were you at Orchard House on 19th June last year?

DAVID: I was.

PROSECUTION: At what time?

DAVID: I cannot give you an exact time, but I think it must have been about 9pm.

PROSECUTION: And when did you leave?

DAVID: It was 9.50pm. I noticed the clock on the dashboard.

PROSECUTION: What were you doing during that time?

DAVID: Firstly, I went to the main house to look around and make sure everything was OK.

PROSECUTION: Passing the Gatekeeper's Cottage?

DAVID: No, when coming from Knutsford, there is a lane off the bypass that goes to the back of the property.

PROSECUTION: I see. Please go on.

DAVID: I had a quick look round, but it was getting dark, and the electricity had been disconnected, so I didn't stay long. It was still pleasant, so I decided to walk down to the cottage; the lane doesn't connect to the main drive, and it is only around a 10-minute' walk.

PROSECUTION: Despite it being dark.

DAVID: It wasn't yet pitch black.

PROSECUTION: Did you see anyone at all?

DAVID: No.

PROSECUTION: Did you hear anything?

DAVID: Yes.

PROSECUTION: What did you hear?

DAVID: A scream.

PROSECUTION: A scream!

DAVID: Yes, followed by a man making an "uh" sound. Like a laugh or a grunt.

PROSECUTION: Didn't that concern you?

DAVID: Not really. It is common for youths from the village to hang around in the woods on the other side of the wall. I assumed it was just horseplay.

PROSECUTION: It didn't occur to you that someone could be calling out in mortal terror.

DAVID: The scream disconcerted me for a moment, but the grunt seemed so natural it reassured me.

PROSECUTION: How far from the cottage were you?

DAVID: A hundred yards or so. The road twists round as you approach it.

PROSECUTION: What did you do when you arrived at the cottage?

DAVID: I popped the key for the main house through the letterbox.

PROSECUTION: You didn't go in?

DAVID: There was no need.

PROSECUTION: You didn't see anyone?

DAVID: No.

PROSECUTION: Is it possible that, if anyone had been inside the cottage, they would have heard you coming?

DAVID: I expect so. It was a very still evening, and I was making quite a noise as I walked on the gravel path.

PROSECUTION: What did you do next?

DAVID: I just returned to my car and went home.

PROSECUTION: Chloe Langton told us that she rang you the following morning to inform you of what she'd found at the cottage. Why didn't you contact the police immediately with all this information?

DAVID: I had no desire to be involved. What information did I have that could possibly be relevant?

PROSECUTION: Quite a lot, I'd imagine. What time did you arrive home?

DAVID: 10.30pm. My wife was just about to go to bed.

PROSECUTION: Did anyone else see you?

DAVID: No.

PROSECUTION: No more questions.

PROSECUTION sits and DEFENCE stands.

DEFENCE: Just one question. Did you see a car in the area? Mr. Bellamy's Volkswagen Golf, for example.

DAVID: No.

DEFENCE: Thank you.

PROSECUTION: Just a moment! You said the road twists. Is it possible that the car was parked out of sight?

DAVID: That is possible.

PROSECUTION: And do you think it likely that a pair of murderers would park their car right outside the cottage?

DEFENCE: Your Honour!

JUDGE: Don't answer that question, Mr. Thorne.

PROSECUTION: Very well, that is all.

DEFENCE: Just to be clear. The question I asked you was, did you see a car and you responded that you did not. Is that correct?

DAVID: Yes.

DEFENCE: Thank you.

PROSECUTION: Please may we have Fiona Biggs?

DAVID exits, and FIONA enters the witness box and takes the oath.

FIONA: I swear by almighty God that the evidence I shall give shall be the truth, the whole truth, and nothing but the truth.

PROSECUTION: Please state your name.

FIONA: Fiona Biggs.

PROSECUTION: A little louder, please. How did you know Charlotte Bellamy?

FIONA: We went to school together. I've known her since I was ten years old.

PROSECUTION: Were you fond of her?

FIONA: Yes, very.

PROSECUTION: Did you also know Patrick Ives?

FIONA: Yes, I knew him pretty well.

PROSECUTION: Were he and Lola close?

FIONA: Oh yes, they saw a lot of each other before he went off to uni.

PROSECUTION: Did you ever express an opinion on this?

FIONA: I once told her that she should be careful with boys like Patrick.

PROSECUTION: What did you mean by that?

FIONA: Well, nothing really. Just…. Well, he seemed like a bit of a waster, and I knew he liked to play poker, and he would frequently have, er, competitions amongst his friends.

PROSECUTION: You mean he gambled.

FIONA: Um, I suppose so.

PROSECUTION: And how did Lola react to this advice?

FIONA: She told me to mind my own business and said she could make up her mind without my help.

PROSECUTION: Did you assume that it was Patrick who was the keener of the two?

FIONA: Yes.

PROSECUTION: And did you assume that they would renew their relationship when Patrick returned from university?

FIONA: Yes, everyone thought that.

PROSECUTION: Were you still close to Lola when Patrick came back from university?

FIONA: No, we hardly saw each other. We had, kind of, drifted apart.

PROSECUTION: Why?

FIONA: She had started to mix with another group of people. Not my friends. Then she started to hang out with Elliot all the time.

PROSECUTION: And, having drifted apart, did you ever drift back again?

FIONA: No.

PROSECUTION: Thank you. That is all.

PROSECUTION sits, and DEFENCE stands.

DEFENCE: I won't keep you long. You say that your close friendship with Lola Bellamy came to an end when she started mixing with a different group of people.

FIONA: Yes.

DEFENCE: Did you have no contact with her at all?

FIONA: We were still friends on social media, and we saw each other a couple of times.

DEFENCE: But she never confided in you if her feelings for Patrick had changed?

FIONA: No.

DEFENCE: Thank you. That is all.

PROSECUTION: Mrs. Margaret Ives, please.

FIONA exits, and MARGARET enters the witness box and takes the oath.

MARGARET: I swear by Almighty God that the evidence I shall give shall be the truth, the whole truth, and nothing but the truth.

PROSECUTION: Mrs. Ives, you are Patrick's mother?

MARGARET: Yes.

PROSECUTION: Did you hear Fiona Biggs' testimony?

MARGARET: There is nothing wrong with my hearing.

PROSECUTION: (*Kindly.*) Yes or no, please.

MARGARET: Yes.

PROSECUTION: Were you aware of the affection that Patrick had for Lola before he went away to university?

MARGARET: I knew that they were seeing a lot of each other.

PROSECUTION: Did your son give you any indication of his intentions toward Lola?

MARGARET: He never suggested that they were getting serious.

PROSECUTION: Do you think he would have told you if they were?

MARGARET: Definitely. He tells me everything.

PROSECUTION: Did he tell you that he'd started seeing Lola again, behind Susan's back?

MARGARET: No.

PROSECUTION: Not everything then.

MARGARET: Unless it is untrue.

PROSECUTION: I assure you that there is plenty of evidence that it is true. When did you first come to Chadwick?

MARGARET: Around 15 years ago.

PROSECUTION: You were a widow supporting yourself and young Patrick on your own?

MARGARET: No.

PROSECUTION: No to what?

MARGARET: Both.

PROSECUTION: You mean that your husband was still alive?

MARGARET: I actually have no idea. I know he is dead now, but I don't know when he died. He might have still been alive when I moved to Chadwick. We had been separated for a very long time.

PROSECUTION: You didn't divorce?

MARGARET: No. It wasn't a happy marriage. He left me for another woman not long after Patrick was born, but we never got round to getting divorced.

PROSECUTION: But everyone assumed you were a widow?

MARGARET: Everyone except Patrick. He always knew the truth.

PROSECUTION: You were not getting any support from your ex, er, I mean from your husband?

MARGARET: No. When I said that I didn't have to support us on my own, I meant that Patrick did what he could.

PROSECUTION: I see. If we can turn to the evening of the 19th of June. Where were you?

MARGARET: In the rose garden.

PROSECUTION: Did you see Kathleen Page pass you on her way to the bottom of the garden?

MARGARET: I think so, but I wouldn't have taken much notice.

PROSECUTION: Did you see Susan?

MARGARET: Yes.

PROSECUTION: Where was she going?

MARGARET: Towards the back gate.

PROSECUTION: Could you advise the distance between your house and Orchard House?

MARGARET: About 2 miles by road, but across the road at the back of the house, there is a public footpath across the fields, which must be only about a mile or so. I think it comes out near a summerhouse on the Orchard House estate. I've never seen it myself, but I know that the nanny takes the children there without the permission of their parents, I might add. I told Patrick about it.

PROSECUTION: Did Susan say anything to you as she passed?

MARGARET: Yes, she said that she was going to visit her friend, Lisa, and that Patrick would be going out later to go round to his friend Paul's house to play poker.

PROSECUTION: Did you see her again that evening?

MARGARET: Yes. Minutes after she had left, she ran back into the house. I assumed she must have forgotten something. Then she left again by the back gate.

PROSECUTION: Was that the last time you saw her that evening?

MARGARET: No. She came into my room after I had gone to bed.

PROSECUTION: What time was this?

MARGARET: Well, I go to bed around 10pm and usually read for half an hour. I had just turned off my light when I heard the front door, so that must have been after ten-thirty.

PROSECUTION: Are you sure that it was Susan returning and not Patrick?

MARGARET: Yes, he never got back before midnight if he'd been playing poker. Besides which, as I said, she came into my room.

PROSECUTION: What time was this?

MARGARET: About five minutes after I heard her return.

PROSECUTION: Why did she come into your room?

MARGARET: She had brought me a snack: some fruit. I sleep badly and am often awake in the small hours of the morning. I find it best to get out of bed and do something such as read or knit, for example. Patrick has got into the habit of bringing me a snack before he goes to bed in case I'm peckish. It has become a little ritual.

PROSECUTION: Patrick, not Susan?

MARGARET: Usually, yes, but Susan must have remembered that Patrick was out, so she kindly did it herself.

PROSECUTION: Was she dressed the same as before?

MARGARET: Yes, apart from the fact that she had taken her coat off.

PROSECUTION: Did you speak to her?

MARGARET: Of course. I asked her if Lisa was well.

PROSECUTION: And what was her reply?

MARGARET: She said that she ended up not going to Lisa's. Stephen Bellamy had driven by in his car and offered to give her a lift. But then she checked her phone and realised that Lisa had not read her message and thought it best not to turn up unannounced.

PROSECUTION: Why would that be a problem?

MARGARET: I didn't ask.

PROSECUTION: So, what did she do instead?

MARGARET: They just drove around for a bit, then Stephen dropped her back home.

PROSECUTION: I assume that the fruit she brought you would have been in the kitchen.

MARGARET: Yes.

PROSECUTION: Where will Susan have had the opportunity to wash her hands?

MARGARET: Well, of course.

PROSECUTION: That is all.

PROSECUTION sits, and DEFENCE stands.

DEFENCE: Did Susan seem herself when she brought you the fruit, Mrs. Ives?

MARGARET: Yes.

DEFENCE: Not agitated at all?

MARGARET: No.

DEFENCE: You were asked if Patrick confided in you that he was having an affair. Did he ever mention that he was unhappy?

MARGARET: Never.

DEFENCE: What was your impression of the marriage?

MARGARET: They seemed like the happiest couple in the world.

DEFENCE: Thank you. No more questions.

PROSECUTION: Call Elliot Forrester, please.

MARGARET exits, and ELLIOT enters the witness box and takes the oath.

ELLIOT: I do solemnly, sincerely, and truly declare and affirm that the evidence I shall give shall be the truth, the whole truth, and nothing but the truth.

PROSECUTION: Please state your name.

ELLIOT: Elliot Forrester

PROSECUTION: Mr. Forrester, where were you on the afternoon of June 19th last year?

ELLIOT: At the cricket club.

PROSECUTION: What were you doing there?

ELLIOT: There was a match on. I didn't have a great innings but hung around having a few drinks and chatting.

PROSECUTION: Did you see Susan Ives?

ELLIOT: Yes.

PROSECUTION: Did you talk to her?

ELLIOT: Yes.

PROSECUTION: What did you say?

ELLIOT: Do I have to answer that?

JUDGE: I'm afraid you do.

ELLIOT: Oh, all right. I told her that she ought to keep an eye on her husband.

PROSECUTION: Why did you tell her that?

ELLIOT: Because I knew that he was seeing Lola.

PROSECUTION: Do you mean that you knew they were meeting in secret?

ELLIOT: Yes, that's it. They were meeting at the cottage of Orchard House.

PROSECUTION: How did you know that?

ELLIOT: Daz told me.

PROSECUTION: Who is Daz?

ELLIOT: He's a kind of handyman. Does a bit of work for the Bellamys.

PROSECUTION: His full name is Darren York. Is that correct?

ELLIOT: That's it.

PROSECUTION: How did he come to tell you of these meetings?

ELLIOT: I'd seen Lola catching the bus from just outside her house on a few occasions, and I told Daz I'd give him £20 to find out where she went. He told me he already knew.

PROSECUTION: How did he know?

ELLIOT: Because he does work at Orchard House as well and has a key for the cottage. She asked to borrow the key, telling him some rubbish about wanting to practice the piano there.

PROSECUTION: There is a piano in the Gatekeeper's Cottage?

ELLIOT: I suppose there must be.

PROSECUTION: Do you know when she last borrowed the key?

ELLIOT: Yes. Before lunch on 19th June last year. Daz sent me a message to say that she'd asked for the key and gone out in the car.

PROSECUTION: What did you do?

ELLIOT: I went round to the cottage.

PROSECUTION: Was she there?

ELLIOT: No.

PROSECUTION: How do you know?

ELLIOT: There was no car. And no one playing the piano.

PROSECUTION: What did you do then?

ELLIOT: I had a smoke, then left for the cricket club.

PROSECUTION: Were you involved in the match?

ELLIOT: Yes. I wasn't sure we'd get a game, but the weather cleared, and we had a shortened match. The other side batted first, and then I didn't last long when it was my turn, so I just went to hang around the clubhouse.

PROSECUTION: Who did you see there?

ELLIOT: The usual lot. Lola was there, Suzie, Rich Burrows, Lisa Langton and her fella, Paul Harrison and his missus. Stephen plays for the other side, so he was out on the field.

PROSECUTION: This is when you told Susan Ives about her husband having an affair?

ELLIOT: Yes.

PROSECUTION: Was Patrick Ives there?

ELLIOT: No, I think he had to go into his office.

PROSECUTION: What made you tell Susan?

ELLIOT: I thought she had a right to know.

PROSECUTION: Had you been drinking?

ELLIOT: Well, yes. I had a couple beforehand because I didn't think we'd get a game. Then I had a couple afterwards to drown my sorrows at how badly I'd played!

PROSECUTION: What did Susan say?

ELLIOT: She told me she didn't believe it, but I said I'd seen them with my own eyes.

PROSECUTION: Then what happened?

ELLIOT: The game ended; Paul Harrison came over, and we decided to all go back to Suzie's.

PROSECUTION: Did you talk about it again at the Ives's house?

ELLIOT: No, except when I was about to leave, Suzie came up to me and asked me not to mention it to anyone else until she had decided what to do.

PROSECUTION: You then went home?

ELLIOT: Yes.

PROSECUTION: You share a property with Richard Burrows. Is that correct?

ELLIOT: Yes.

PROSECUTION: Were you together that evening?

ELLIOT: No. We were supposed to be going round to Paul's to play poker, but I'd got a rotten headache, so Rich went on his own.

PROSECUTION: What time was this?

ELLIOT: Probably about 8.45. He was due at Paul's at 9pm.

PROSECUTION: And what did you do?

ELLIOT: Watched a bit of TV but couldn't be bothered with anything, so decided to have a smoke and go to bed. That's when I realised I didn't have my lighter. I must have dropped it at the cottage.

PROSECUTION: What time was this?

ELLIOT: About nine-thirty.

PROSECUTION: Was there anything special about that lighter?

ELLIOT: Not really, but it had my name on it, and I didn't want anyone to know I'd been hanging around the cottage.

PROSECUTION: Why did it have your name on it?

ELLIOT: It was a present from Lola. From back in the day.

PROSECUTION: Did you go out to look for it?

ELLIOT: I couldn't be bothered. I sent Rich a text asking him to pick up a disposable from the garage on the way home.

PROSECUTION: Then you went to bed.

ELLIOT: No. I was annoyed that I couldn't smoke. I put the TV back on and was asleep on the sofa when Rich came back around 11.30.

PROSECUTION: Thank you, that is all.

PROSECUTION sits, and DEFENCE stands.

DEFENCE: Could you describe the lighter for us?

ELLIOT: It is black and silver. The type with a button on the top, which ignites the flame.

DEFENCE: Has it been suggested to you that the discovery of that lighter at the cottage could be useful to the defence?

ELLIOT: Not that I remember.

DEFENCE: What car do you drive, Mr. Forrester?

ELLIOT: A Range Rover.

DEFENCE: You mentioned that you'd had a few drinks before you told Susan Ives that her husband was having an affair. Do you remember how many?

ELLIOT: Three or four, I suppose.

DEFENCE: Three or four after your innings and several before?

ELLIOT: Possibly.

DEFENCE: Would you have spoken to Susan in this way had you not been drinking?

ELLIOT: I have no idea.

DEFENCE: What did you hope would be gained from you passing on this information?

ELLIOT: I hoped she'd put a stop to it.

DEFENCE: With a knife?

ELLIOT: What! Of course not. I thought she'd tell him to stop seeing Lola.

DEFENCE: It was important to you that he stopped, wasn't it?

ELLIOT: I don't know what you mean.

DEFENCE: I think you do. You had been trying to persuade Lola to leave Stephen and move in with you, hadn't you? (*Pause.*) Hadn't you?

ELLIOT: Yes.

DEFENCE: How long had you had this affection for Lola?

ELLIOT: Since we were teenagers. She…

DEFENCE: Take your time, Mr. Forrester.

ELLIOT: She broke my heart, but I never stopped loving her.

DEFENCE: Did she end the relationship with you?

ELLIOT: Yes.

DEFENCE: What was the reason?

ELLIOT: She said I'd never get anywhere in life.

DEFENCE: Her reasons were financial?

PROSECUTION: Your Honour.

DEFENCE: I withdraw the question. Do you consider yourself to be a stalker, Mr. Forrester?

ELLIOT: Of course not.

DEFENCE: So, why were you hanging around her property to see her getting on the bus "on several occasions"?

ELLIOT: Their place is on the main road. I just happened to be passing.

DEFENCE: Is that so? Her affair with Patrick was good news for you, wasn't it? If you could make it public and, at the same time, put a stop to it, you thought Stephen would divorce her and clear the path for you. You must have been very pleased with yourself having finally plucked up the courage to tell Susan and put the wheels in motion.

ELLIOT: No.

DEFENCE: When you went home on 19th June last year, you cracked open a bottle of single malt to celebrate, didn't you?

ELLIOT: I had a drink, yes.

DEFENCE: You drank three quarters of the bottle. Are you sure that you didn't notice your lighter missing until 9.30?

ELLIOT: Yes.

DEFENCE: How do you know?

ELLIOT: Because I messaged Rich at 9.45. I'd only spent a few minutes looking for it.

DEFENCE: Didn't you send that message to give the impression that you were at home, that you hadn't been out since he had left when, in fact, you'd driven to the cottage and failed in your search for the lighter?

ELLIOT: No. That's ridiculous.

DEFENCE: Weren't you, in fact, at the cottage at nine-thirty that evening?

ELLIOT: No.

DEFENCE: (*Pause.*) When did you hear about the murder?

ELLIOT: Oh. It was late Sunday morning. 11.30, maybe. Paul rang me to tell me. I could hardly believe what he was telling me.

DEFENCE: But you believed it enough to go into the bathroom and grab a handful of your housemate's prescription medicine, wanting to end your life, didn't you?

ELLIOT: Oh, God.

DEFENCE: And you might have succeeded had he not forced his way in and knocked them out of your hand. Do you remember what you said to him?

ELLIOT: No, I…

DEFENCE: You said, and I quote, "Get away from me, Rich. After what I've done, I cannot go on."

ELLIOT: I don't remember.

DEFENCE: Elliot Forrester, were you at Orchard House gatekeeper's cottage at around 9.30pm on the 19th of June last year?

ELLIOT: No.

DEFENCE: Was it your grunt that David Thorne heard coming from the cottage?

PROSECUTION: (*Jumping up.*) Really, Your Honour, Mr. Forrester is not on trial here.

DEFENCE: No further questions. (*He sits.*)

PROSECUTION: I have. Elliot, do you regret telling Susan about her husband's affair with Lola?

ELLIOT: Yes, I do. I shouldn't have said anything.

PROSECUTION: Was that why you attempted suicide when you heard that Lola had been murdered?

ELLIOT: Yes.

PROSECUTION: No further questions. Please call Paul Harrison.

ELLIOT exits, and PAUL enters the witness box and takes the oath.

PAUL: I do solemnly, sincerely, and truly declare and affirm that the evidence I shall give shall be the truth, the whole truth, and nothing but the truth.

PROSECUTION: Mr. Harrison, did you have some friends round to play poker on the night of June 19th last year?

PAUL: Yes, I did.

PROSECUTION: Were you present when Richard Burrows received the text message from Elliot Forrester?

PAUL: I was.

PROSECUTION: Did Richard comment on the text that he received?

PAUL: Yes, he said, "The idiot wants me to pick up a ciggie lighter on the way home," or words to that effect.

PROSECUTION: And what time did Richard leave?

PAUL: At around 11.45.

PROSECUTION: Did you call Elliot the following day around noon?

PAUL: Yes.

PROSECUTION: What was the conversation?

PAUL: I told him that something terrible had happened. Lola's body had been found in the Gatekeeper's Cottage at Orchard House, and the police were treating it as murder. He just kept saying, "No, Paul, no, don't."

PROSECUTION: He seemed shocked?

PAUL: He seemed absolutely speechless.

PROSECUTION: No further questions.

PROSECUTION sits, and DEFENCE stands.

DEFENCE: Did anyone else hear Mr. Burrows' remark about the text message?

PAUL: I'm sure everyone heard.

DEFENCE: Who is everyone?

PAUL: Well, besides myself and Rich, there was my friend Steve, two colleagues from work, er, let me think.

DEFENCE: Wasn't Patrick Ives in the room?

PAUL: Patrick? No.

DEFENCE: What time did he arrive?

PAUL: Well, he didn't.

DEFENCE: He wasn't there all evening?

PAUL: No.

DEFENCE: Did he let you know he wasn't coming?

PAUL: No. He, er, just didn't turn up.

DEFENCE: Thank you. No further questions.

PROSECUTION: Call Melanie Cooper.

PAUL exits, and MELANIE enters the witness box and takes the oath.

MELANIE: I swear by Almighty God that the evidence I shall give shall be the truth, the whole truth, and nothing but the truth.

PROSECUTION: Ms. Cooper, you are a cleaner at the Ives' residence?

MELANIE: No, I'm a housekeeper. I do much more than just clean.

PROSECUTION: My apologies. What are your hours?

MELANIE: Three days a week. More if required.

PROSECUTION: How did you come to be employed by the Ives's?

MELANIE: I used to do one morning a week for Lola Bellamy for a while, but I think they were struggling a bit. Rather than just let me go, Lola was kind enough to recommend me to Susan Ives.

PROSECUTION: Are you still employed by the Ives's?

MELANIE: No. I resigned on June 20th last year.

PROSECUTION: Was that related to the death of Lola?

MELANIE: Yes.

PROSECUTION: Are you familiar with a book with the title Commercial Management: Theory and Practice by the author David Lowe?

MELANIE: I am.

PROSECUTION: How do you know it?

MELANIE: There is a copy in Patrick's study.

PROSECUTION: When did you last see it?

MELANIE: June 20th last year.

PROSECUTION: What made you look at it?

MELANIE: I wanted to see if the note I put in it was still there.

PROSECUTION: Was it?

MELANIE: No.

PROSECUTION: For whom was the note intended?

MELANIE: Patrick

PROSECUTION: From you?

MELANIE: No. From Lola.

PROSECUTION: How did you come to be in possession of a note intended for Patrick from Lola?

MELANIE: She had been giving me notes to pass on for about six months or so. She said that she didn't trust email.

PROSECUTION: What do you think she meant by that?

MELANIE: That the notes were private.

PROSECUTION: Did you read them?

MELANIE: No. She sealed them inside an envelope, but I wouldn't have read them anyway.

PROSECUTION: At what time did you place the note in the book on the 19th of June?

MELANIE: About 6.45pm.

PROSECUTION: Was that the usual time?

MELANIE: No, I would normally do it in the morning when I was cleaning the study, but Margaret Ives was in there with Laura on and off all day. It was marked urgent, so I didn't want to leave it until the following morning, but by half past six I was worried that someone might ask why I hadn't yet finished for the day, so I took my chance whilst the study was empty.

PROSECUTION: So, you were able to do it unobserved?

MELANIE: I thought so, but as I turned to come out of the room, I saw Susan and Elliot in the hallway. I moved to one side until they had gone. I heard Elliot leave by the front door.

PROSECUTION: Did they see you?

MELANIE: I don't know. It was Elliot who was facing me, but there is a mirror in the hall, so Susan might have seen me as well.

PROSECUTION: As you waited for them to go, could you hear what they were saying?

MELANIE: No, they were whispering.

PROSECUTION: What happened after that?

MELANIE: Once the coast was clear, I went home.

PROSECUTION: But you were back the next day.

MELANIE: Yes. Sometimes they fancied having a big, cooked breakfast on a Sunday, and I'd go in to prepare it for them.

PROSECUTION: Did anything unusual occur?

MELANIE: Not at breakfast, but afterwards I saw Patrick coming out of the study, and I asked him if he'd seen the note.

PROSECUTION: Had he?

MELANIE: No. He said it wasn't there.

PROSECUTION: Thank you. That will be all.

PROSECUTION sits, and DEFENCE stands.

DEFENCE: Ms. Cooper, you must be perfectly aware that, if Susan Ives discovered you passing secret notes to her husband, she would have sacked you without question.

MELANIE: I know that she has a temper.

DEFENCE: So, you resigned before she had the chance.

MELANIE: No. As I said, I left because Lola had been murdered.

DEFENCE: You also said that, whilst you were spying on Susan and Elliot, you heard him leave by the front door. How did you know it was him?

MELANIE: Who else would it be?

DEFENCE: It could be any one of a number of people. The fact is, you don't know whether he left the house or not.

MELANIE: I suppose.

DEFENCE: No further questions.

PROSECUTION: Please call Laura Roberts.

MELANIE exits, and LAURA enters the witness box and takes the oath.

LAURA: I swear by Almighty God that the evidence I shall give shall be the truth, the whole truth, and nothing but the truth.

PROSECUTION: Mrs. Roberts. Where were you living in June of last year?

LAURA: Well, my home is on the Isle of Wight, but Margaret had been kind enough to invite me to stay with her for a few weeks.

PROSECUTION: You are old friends?

LAURA: We've known each other for donkey's years. I knew her before she moved to Chadwick.

PROSECUTION: Did you spend the evening of 19th June in the rose garden with Margaret Ives?

LAURA: No, I was feeling a little under the weather, so I spent the evening in my room.

PROSECUTION: Where is your room?

LAURA: On the top floor.

PROSECUTION: You were there all evening?

LAURA: Yes, apart from when I went down to get a glass of water.

PROSECUTION: What time was this?

LAURA: Around 8.30.

PROSECUTION: You are sure of this?

LAURA: Yes, I glanced at the clock because I had been snoozing.

PROSECUTION: What happened when you left your room?

LAURA: I heard voices and crying from Kathleen Page's room. I tried the door, but it was locked. I asked if everything was ok, and after a moment, Kathleen said that she was all right but just had a bit of a headache. I didn't believe her, though; I've never heard crying like it.

PROSECUTION: You were mistaken about hearing voices, though. It was just Kathleen crying.

LAURA: Oh, no. I heard the voice quite distinctly. It was Patrick.

PROSECUTION: You are sure it was Patrick?

LAURA: Yes.

PROSECUTION: Could you hear what he was saying?

LAURA: No.

PROSECUTION: (*After a pause.*) Now then. I believe you used to run the odd errand for the family.

LAURA: Yes, I liked to make myself useful in return for their kindness.

PROSECUTION: Did Susan Ives ask you to do something for her on Sunday, 20th June last year?

LAURA: Yes. She gave me a bag of clothes to put in the recycling bin at Sainsbury's in Wilmslow.

PROSECUTION: Was there anything unusual about this?

LAURA: No, she knew that I would be going to church and that I'd park in Sainsbury's car park. She was very generous about giving away unwanted clothes.

PROSECUTION: You went to church on your own.

LAURA: Yes. They are not a religious family. Margaret used to go, years ago, but she doesn't bother anymore.

PROSECUTION: Did you see what was in the bag?

LAURA: There were a couple of jumpers, a dress, a blouse…

PROSECUTION: Anything else?

LAURA: A coat.

PROSECUTION: Can you describe it?

LAURA: It was her summer coat. Sort of biscuit-coloured.

PROSECUTION: She was throwing out her summer coat in summer.

LAURA: She said she'd got oil stains on it from Stephen Bellamy's car. I said that they would clean out, but she said she was tired of it anyway.

PROSECUTION: Did you see the oil stains?

LAURA: No, she'd wrapped the coat in another bag.

PROSECUTION: Are you not supposed to take clothes out of any bags when you place them in these recycling bins?

LAURA: Yes, but she said not to because the oil would contaminate the other clothing.

PROSECUTION: So, you didn't actually see the coat.

LAURA: No.

PROSECUTION: And there were no identifying marks on the bag to show where it had come from.

LAURA: Why would there be?

PROSECUTION: Quite. No further questions.

PROSECUTION sits, and DEFENCE stands.

DEFENCE: No questions.

PROSECUTION: Call Darren York.

LAURA exits, and DARREN enters the witness box and takes the oath.

DARREN: I do solemnly, sincerely, and truly declare and affirm that the evidence I shall give shall be the truth, the whole truth, and nothing but the truth.

PROSECUTION: You are Darren York.

DARREN: Yes.

PROSECUTION: And you do work for Mr. and Mrs. Bellamy.

DARREN: Not anymore. He's in prison, and she's dead.

PROSECUTION: But you did work for them before the events of June last year?

DARREN: Yeah, as and when.

PROSECUTION: What did you do?

DARREN: Anything that needed doing.

PROSECUTION: You're a kind of handyman.

DARREN: That's it.

PROSECUTION: What were you doing on 19th June last year?

DARREN: Repairing the front fence. Again.

PROSECUTION: Did you send Elliot Forrester a text to say that Lola Bellamy had borrowed the key for the Gatekeepers Cottage about noon that day?

DARREN: Yes.

PROSECUTION: Did he reply?

DARREN: Yes, he said he'd go to check it out.

PROSECUTION: When did you last see Lola?

DARREN: About eight o'clock that night.

PROSECUTION: You were still working on the fence at that time?

DARREN: I work whenever there's work to be done.

PROSECUTION: Did she speak to you?

DARREN: Yes, she said I ought to get myself off and gave me a fiver for a drink.

PROSECUTION: Did she take the money out of her bag?

DARREN: Yes.

PROSECUTION: Did you see anything else in the bag?

DARREN: Yes, what looked like three or four letters.

PROSECUTION: And you never saw her again?

DARREN: Never.

PROSECUTION: Mr. York, did you sometimes do a bit of work on Stephen Bellamy's car?

DARREN: From time to time.

PROSECUTION: When did you last do anything?

DARREN: About a month before the murder. I changed a tyre.

PROSECUTION: So, you know what tyres were on the car in June last year.

DARREN: Yes, he's got three Bridgestones, two on the back and one on the front, and the other front one is a Maxxis, which is the one I put on for him. The spare is an Ajax.

PROSECUTION: You are sure that the Ajax wasn't on the car.

DARREN: No, it was definitely the spare.

PROSECUTION: Did you see Stephen Bellamy later that evening?

DARREN: Yes, I had just come out of the pub when the car sped past me.

PROSECUTION: What time was this?

DARREN: Nearly ten. I'd decided to have an early night.

PROSECUTION: Was he on his own?

DARREN: No, Susan Ives was in the passenger seat.

PROSECUTION: You are sure of this?

DARREN: Oh, definite. She stared right at me like she'd seen a ghost.

PROSECUTION: Thank you, that is all.

PROSECUTION sits, and DEFENCE stands.

DEFENCE: Mr. York. Did you notice what Lola was wearing when you saw her at around 8pm?

DARREN: Yes, a white dress, er, a dark coat.

DEFENCE: Was she wearing jewellery?

DARREN: Well, she had on her necklace and her rings. She always wore them.

DEFENCE: Do you think they were valuable?

DARREN: I know they were. One time I went into her kitchen while she was washing up, and the rings were on the side, so I told her to be careful she didn't lose them. She said they were insured for so much that if she did, she'd be able to buy a new car!

DEFENCE: Did you ever wonder if Lola's story about using the cottage for piano practice might be untrue?

DARREN: Well, of course. I'm not an idiot. She only ever went there in the evening, and that was when Stephen was away on business. That meant that she had to catch the bus because he always took the car. I'll be honest. One evening, I'd nothing to do, so I took a stroll by the cottage myself on an evening she'd borrowed the key.

DEFENCE: What did you see?

DARREN: Not much, but I didn't hear any music coming from inside.

DEFENCE: Mr. York, you are not very well off, are you?

DARREN: As poor as a church mouse, as my mum would have said, but I get by.

DEFENCE: Aren't you maxed out on your credit cards and owe three months' rent? (*No response.*) Are you familiar with court proceedings?

DARREN: What do you mean?

DEFENCE: Have you ever appeared in court before?

DARREN: Well. Yes.

DEFENCE: Yes. But not in the witness stand. You've been in prison, haven't you?

DARREN: Yes.

DEFENCE: Ten months for robbery, is that correct?

DARREN: Yes. It was a long time ago. I did my time.

PROSECUTION: Might I ask what on earth this has to do with the murder of Susan Bellamy?

JUDGE: Well?

DEFENCE: I am trying to establish that Mr. York has a reputation and motive for robbery.

PROSECUTION: Precisely.

JUDGE: Mr. York is not on trial.

DEFENCE: In that case, no further questions, Your Honour.

PROSECUTION: Please call Joanne Trimble.

DARREN exits, and JOANNE enters the witness box and takes the oath.

JOANNE: I swear by Almighty God that the evidence I shall give shall be the truth, the whole truth, and nothing but the truth.

PROSECUTION: Please describe your occupation.

JOANNE: I'm a bus driver.

PROSECUTION: Do you have a regular route?

JOANNE: Number 37, Crewe to Macclesfield.

PROSECUTION: And this takes you past both the Bellamy residence and Orchard House?

JOANNE: Yes.

PROSECUTION: Did you know Lola Bellamy?

JOANNE: I know who she is now, but not at the time, no.

PROSECUTION: The time being the 19th of June last year.

JOANNE: Yes.

PROSECUTION: Was that the first time she'd caught your bus?

JOANNE: No, she'd caught it a few times, always at the same time.

PROSECUTION: You remember her?

JOANNE: Yes, because the stops outside Orchard House are in the middle of nowhere, really. I don't know why they are there; nobody ever gets on or off, especially in the evening.

PROSECUTION: What is the distance between the stop where she got on and Orchard House?

JOANNE: About three miles. It is timed at eight minutes due to the speed limit and the narrowness of the road.

PROSECUTION: Can you be sure you saw her on June 19th?

JOANNE: Yes, I heard about the murder the next day and contacted the police to say I'd seen her.

PROSECUTION: How did she seem?

JOANNE: Agitated. She was waiting by the door as I slowed down and ran down the lane to Orchard House.

PROSECUTION: Thank you. I have no further questions.

PROSECUTION sits, and DEFENCE stands.

DEFENCE: No questions.

PROSECUTION: Call Sergeant Calvert.

JOANNE exits, and CALVERT enters the witness box and takes the oath.

CALVERT: I swear by Almighty God that the evidence I shall give shall be the truth, the whole truth, and nothing but the truth.

PROSECUTION: You are a police sergeant stationed at Wilmslow.

CALVERT: Yes.

PROSECUTION: Were you asked to attend the scene at the Gatekeeper's Cottage?

CALVERT: Yes, it came over the radio.

PROSECUTION: You drove straight there?

CALVERT: Yes.

PROSECUTION: And parked outside the cottage.

CALVERT: No, a little further back.

PROSECUTION: Why was that?

CALVERT: The ground is soft outside the cottage, so I stayed back in case there were any tyre marks that might be useful to the inquiry.

PROSECUTION: And were there?

CALVERT: Yes. At least four sets, two from the same car.

PROSECUTION: They were quite clear.

CALVERT: Some were. There had been a heavy storm around lunchtime on the 19th, so the ground was soft for the rest of the day. If we label the prints A, B1, B2, and C, then B1 and B2 were quite distinct.

PROSECUTION: What can you tell us about the prints?

CALVERT: Well, A was made by a large, heavy car, but it must have been before the storm because any distinguishing marks had been washed away. C was a light imprint, meaning the ground had dried out, and I assumed these were made by the estate agent.

PROSECUTION: What about B1 and B2?

CALVERT: Definitely from the same car. We were able to take casts and ascertain that two of the tyres, the right front and rear left, were very worn, but the left front and right rear were brand new or, at least, nearly brand new.

PROSECUTION: Were you able to ascertain the makes of those new tyres?

CALVERT: Yes. The front one was Maxxis, and the rear was Ajax.

PROSECUTION: Do the tyres match any of the vehicles involved in this case?

CALVERT: Yes, they match exactly with Stephen Bellamy's Volkswagen Golf.

PROSECUTION: You have examined the car?

CALVERT: Of course, we picked it up on the 20th.

PROSECUTION: Was there any oil or grease on the bodywork?

CALVERT: No.

PROSECUTION: Did you find anything of interest around the cottage?

CALVERT: Yes, we found a discarded water bottle.

PROSECUTION: Has it ever been identified as being someone's property?

CALVERT: No.

PROSECUTION: Might it have been there a long time?

CALVERT: I don't think so; it was quite clean.

PROSECUTION: Did you find Lola Bellamy's bag inside the cottage?

CALVERT: I did.

PROSECUTION: Did it contain some letters?

CALVERT: Yes, there were three envelopes addressed to Ms. Bellamy.

PROSECUTION: Thank you, that is all.

PROSECUTION sits and DEFENCE stands.

DEFENCE: Were there any tyre tracks at the rear of the cottage?

CALVERT: No.

DEFENCE: None at all?

CALVERT: No.

DEFENCE: That is all.

PROSECUTION: Thank you, Sergeant Calvert, you may go.

CALVERT exits.

PROSECUTION: With permission, I'd like to read out the letters found in Lola Bellamy's bag.

JUDGE: Any opposition?

DEFENCE: Are they relevant?

JUDGE: The prosecution obviously believes them to be. Do you have any reasonable grounds to object?

DEFENCE: No.

JUDGE: In that case, you may proceed.

PROSECUTION: The first is dated May 21st. "My darling. I waited for you for an hour and then got home to find that horrible note. How can you say you don't love me? I know it isn't true, and you know that I have never loved anyone else. Please don't tell me it is over. Meet me tomorrow at 9. I will find a way to get away." This is followed by the initial P. The next is dated June 8th and reads, "Oh, my precious. It is 4am, and I haven't slept a wink. Who needs sleep when I have you? You are my sun, my moon, my stars, my everything. I love you, my beautiful sweetheart. P." The last one is dated June 9th. "I went to bed as soon as I got home like you said, but it did me no good. How can I ever sleep again, now that I have you? Don't be afraid, my darling. Things will be tough for a while, but then we will be together forever. P."

JUDGE: That's all the letters?

PROSECUTION: Yes, and I had hoped to rest the case for the prosecution there, but, unfortunately, I still have one witness to call who has been unavoidably detained due to a flight cancellation. This is a very important witness and must be called, so can I suggest we rise until they attend?

DEFENCE: Your Honour, this doesn't seem very fair to my witnesses who are waiting their turn. How long must they be kept waiting?

PROSECUTION: That is difficult to say, but the only alternative would be to begin the case for the defence and then call my witness when they are available.

JUDGE: An unusual suggestion, but I will allow it if there are no objections.

DEFENCE: Very well.

JUDGE: In that case, let us take a break, and you can begin the case for defence after we've had some refreshments.

USHER: Court rise.

END OF ACT ONE

ACT TWO

The same.

USHER: Court rise. (*All rise and the JUDGE enters.*)

JUDGE: Please be seated (*All sit.*) The case for the defence.

DEFENCE: Thank you, Your Honour. Call Stephen Bellamy, please.

STEPHEN enters the witness box and takes the oath.

STEPHEN: I swear by Almighty God that the evidence I shall give shall be the truth, the whole truth, and nothing but the truth.

DEFENCE: Mr. Bellamy, could you tell us where you were at 9.30pm on 19th June last year?

STEPHEN: Yes, I was in my car, driving back to Chadwick from Astbury Mere.

DEFENCE: Astbury Mere is nowhere near Orchard House?

STEPHEN: It is about 12 miles from there.

DEFENCE: Was anyone with you?

STEPHEN: Yes, Suzie. Susan Ives.

DEFENCE: You are sure of the time?

STEPHEN: Yes.

DEFENCE: What time did you leave Chadwick Cricket Club earlier that day?

STEPHEN: I think it was just before six.

DEFENCE: Did you notice Elliot Forrester in conversation with Susan Ives before you left?

STEPHEN: Yes, I made a joke about it. I said to Lola, "It looks like Elliot has found himself a new girlfriend, you are off the hook."

DEFENCE: You knew of his obsession with your wife?

STEPHEN: Yes, it was a bit of a joke, but could be annoying sometimes.

DEFENCE: You didn't imagine that there could be anything in it?

STEPHEN: No.

DEFENCE: Did you think it possible that your wife might be having an affair with anyone?

STEPHEN: Not for a second. I thought we were happy. I thought she loved me.

DEFENCE: I'm sorry if I've upset you. What time did you go to bed that evening?

STEPHEN: I didn't. I was up all night with worry.

DEFENCE: Of course. Could you tell us what happened that evening from you leaving the cricket club until, say 11pm?

STEPHEN: I will do my best. I have a few problems with my memory. On the way home from the cricket, Lola said she was going round to her friend, Lisa's, house after dinner. I offered to take her, but she said that she wanted to have the car in case they decided to take off anywhere. I said, it was fine, I'd drop her off then walk back. After dinner, I went out to the car and Lola pointed out that I'd got a flat tyre. She said not to worry, she'd walk to Lisa's and someone else would have to drive if necessary. So, I set about changing the tyre.

DEFENCE: Were you able to identify why it was flat?

STEPHEN: Yes, there was a cut in the side wall.

DEFENCE: Isn't that a bit unusual?

STEPHEN: I suppose so. I don't know much about tyres.

DEFENCE: What happened next?

STEPHEN: I'd just got the tyre off when Suzie rang asking if Lola was there. I told her she'd gone to Lisa Langton's and she asked if I was sure that was where she'd gone. I said of course, then Suzie said she needed to see me at once. Something that she couldn't discuss on the phone. Then she asked me to pick her up at the back gate to her property. Oh, and she asked me if Elliot had said anything to me.

DEFENCE: What did you do?

STEPHEN: Well, Suzie rather spooked me so, I rang Lola to check that she was ok, but it went to voicemail, mobile reception is very patchy around where we live, so I called Lisa on her home phone to ask if Lola was there. She was a bit surprised because she wasn't expecting her until after eight-thirty and it was only just after eight. Then, I got the tyre on as quick as I could and drove to the back of Suzie's.

DEFENCE: And she was waiting for you?

STEPHEN: Yes. I said, "What's happened to Lola?" She said, "What do you mean, what's happened?" I told her that she wasn't at Lisa's, and she said, "So, Elliot was right." Then she told me that Lola had gone to meet Patrick at Orchard House. I felt like I'd been struck by lightning.

DEFENCE: Were you driving as she told you this?

STEPHEN: Yes, I carried on down the lane toward Congleton.

DEFENCE: What else did Susan Ives tell you?

STEPHEN: She told me that Lola and Patrick were having an affair and had been meeting at Orchard House Gatekeeper's Cottage for the last few weeks. Elliot had seen them there. I asked if she was there with Patrick now and she said no, Patrick had not gone to meet her on this occasion. That there had been some sort of slip up with the arrangement. We'd reached Astbury by now, I wasn't really heading anywhere in particular, but we ended up there more or less by accident. I said that I wanted to head back to Chadwick, but I'd need to put some petrol in first, so we went to the Tesco petrol station in Congleton and filled up.

DEFENCE: What time was this?

STEPHEN: About twenty past nine.

DEFENCE: Did you pay by card?

STEPHEN: Yes, my debit card.

DEFENCE: How far is it to Orchard House from Congleton?

STEPHEN: About a thirty-minute drive.

DEFENCE: What happened when you got back to Chadwick?

STEPHEN: I drove to Lisa Langton's but felt a bit embarrassed so, instead of knocking on the door, I rang from my car and asked for Lola. Lisa told me that Lola hadn't turned up. I was all set to go to the Gatekeeper's Cottage, but Suzie reminded me that Patrick had not kept the appointment and there was no way that Lola would still be waiting for him at that time, so I went straight home but Lola was not there either. I was frantic by now. I rang Wilmslow police and the A&E at Macclesfield, I drove back to Lisa's, then back home again hoping to see some sign but there was nothing. Eventually we agreed there was nothing that we could do, and I took Suzie home.

DEFENCE: What time was this?

STEPHEN: It will have been about a quarter to eleven.

DEFENCE: Did you go to the rear gate?

STEPHEN: No, to the front. Suzie said that she would confirm that Patrick was still there by turning the porch light on and off twice.

DEFENCE: Which she did?

STEPHEN: Yes.

DEFENCE: What did you do then?

STEPHEN: My head was spinning. I drove around for a bit then went home.

DEFENCE: Just to be clear. You are absolutely sure that, at the time fixed for the murder, you had only just left Congleton.

STEPHEN: Yes.

DEFENCE: And that it is ten miles from Orchard House.

STEPHEN: More like twelve.

DEFENCE: Thank you. No more questions.

DEFENCE sits and PROSECUTION stands.

PROSECUTION: If we can go back to earlier in the evening when you got home from the cricket club. Who cooked dinner that night?

STEPHEN: I did.

PROSECUTION: Was Lola in the kitchen with you?

STEPHEN: No.

PROSECUTION: So, she had the opportunity to slip out and make an incision in the car tyre.

STEPHEN: Yes, I suppose she did.

PROSECUTION: She never suggested that you accompany her to Lisa Langton's?

STEPHEN: No.

PROSECUTION: In fact, she discouraged it.

STEPHEN: Yes.

PROSECUTION: Now. I want you to think about this very carefully before you answer. You claim that at 9.30pm you were still on the road from Congleton to Chadwick, coming back the same way that you went.

STEPHEN: Yes.

PROSECUTION: But you must know that there is another route.

STEPHEN: I am aware that there is a bypass, yes.

PROSECUTION: Why didn't you take that road, weren't you in a hurry to get back?

STEPHEN: There is no exit for Chadwick, it would have taken longer.

PROSECUTION: But there is an exit off which there is a back lane that will take you directly to Orchard House.

STEPHEN: Yes, but it is a dead end. It does not connect with the road to the front so wouldn't have made any sense to take it unless the destination was Orchard House.

PROSECUTION: That is precisely my point. Why wasn't Orchard House your destination? You say you were worried about Lola. Wouldn't it have made sense to go directly to the place that Susan Ives had told you she would be?

STEPHEN: I wasn't worried about Lola at that time. I was confident she'd be at Lisa Langton's.

PROSECUTION: So, why didn't you go to Orchard House as soon as you found she wasn't?

STEPHEN: I still didn't believe that she had gone there. And even if she had, Suzie assured me that Patrick hadn't. She wouldn't have waited there for him for so long.

PROSECUTION: So, you did think it possible?

STEPHEN: I just said that I didn't.

PROSECUTION: What reason did Susan Ives give you for her assurance that her husband was at home?

STEPHEN: She didn't give a reason.

PROSECUTION: She didn't mention that a note had been intercepted?

STEPHEN: No.

PROSECUTION: When did you begin to have doubts?

STEPHEN: What do you mean?

PROSECUTION: You asked Susan Ives to confirm that Patrick was home by turning the porch light on and off.

STEPHEN: It was Suzie that suggested that. She knew that I was now getting very worried. I had even said that if Lola and Patrick were at the cottage together at least I'd know she was safe.

PROSECUTION: How very noble of you. What time did you get home after dropping off Mrs. Ives?

STEPHEN: I don't know.

PROSECUTION: You don't know?

STEPHEN: I know that I drove around. I've no idea for how long.

PROSECUTION: Was it after midnight?

STEPHEN: Probably later.

PROSECUTION: After one?

STEPHEN: I think dawn was breaking.

PROSECUTION: Dawn was breaking! Your wife was missing, and it didn't occur to you to go home?

STEPHEN: No.

PROSECUTION: Why not?

STEPHEN: I was out of my mind. I wasn't thinking straight.

PROSECUTION: That's your answer?

STEPHEN: Yes.

PROSECUTION: Let me suggest an alternative. The reason you didn't go to see if your wife had arrived at home is because you knew perfectly well that she was lying dead in a pool of her own blood.

STEPHEN: For God's sake, no!

PROSECUTION: When were you informed of the murder?

STEPHEN: Eleven o'clock on Sunday morning. A police officer came to my house.

PROSECUTION: Were you asked to identify the body?

STEPHEN: Yes. I was taken to the cottage.

PROSECUTION: You identified the body in situ?

STEPHEN: Yes.

PROSECUTION: Was the body to the left or right of the piano?

STEPHEN: The left.

PROSECUTION: Are you sure?

STEPHEN: Yes.

PROSECUTION: I see. (*Pause.*) Mr. Bellamy, when you were taken to the cottage, the body had been moved to the dining room. There is no piano in the dining room, it is across the hall in the room where the body was first discovered. The room where Lola Bellamy was murdered.

STEPHEN: I, I, I must be getting confused.

PROSECUTION: No further questions.

DEFENCE: Nothing more at this stage.

STEPHEN exits.

PROSECUTION: If I may, I would like to call my final witness who was unable to take the stand earlier.

JUDGE: Very well.

PROSECUTION: Please call Dr Gabriel.

DR GABRIEL enters the witness box and takes the oath.

DR GABRIEL: I swear by Almighty God that the evidence I shall give shall be the truth, the whole truth, and nothing but the truth.

PROSECUTION: Please state your profession, Dr Gabriel.

DR GABRIEL: I am a forensic scientist.

PROSECUTION: And what is your speciality?

DR GABRIEL: DNA.

PROSECUTION: How long have you worked in this field?

DR GABRIEL: More than thirty years. I was one of the first forensic scientists to work with the police on DNA identification.

PROSECUTION: Is it possible to obtain a reliable DNA sample from someone touching an object?

DR GABRIEL: Yes.

PROSECUTION: Could you describe, in layman's terms, how that works?

DR GABRIEL: Well, the human body sheds around 400,000 skin cells every day. This is, of course, dead skin, but any sweat on the skin will contain DNA and that will remain on the object.

PROSECUTION: So sweat helps with identification.

DR GABRIEL: Yes.

PROSECUTION: Were you asked to examine some DNA found at the scene of Lola Bellamy's murder?

DR GABRIEL: I was.

PROSECUTION: From where was the sample taken?

DR GABRIEL: It was a fingerprint on the table lamp.

PROSECUTION: Were you able to identify from the DNA who had made that fingerprint?

DR GABRIEL: I was.

PROSECUTION: Who was it?

DR GABRIEL: Susan Ives.

PROSECUTION: There can be no doubt about that.

DR GABRIEL: None whatsoever.

PROSECUTION: Thank you. That is all.

PROSECUTION sits and DEFENCE stands.

DEFENCE: Dr Gabriel, DNA lasts indefinitely, I believe?

DR GABRIEL: That's not true. When exposed to the environment, touch DNA, as found in a fingerprint, will erode over time.

DEFENCE: How long?

DR GABRIEL: About a month before it becomes unreliable.

DEFENCE: So, that fingerprint could have been made at any time in the previous month.

DR GABRIEL: Yes.

DEFENCE: Was any other DNA from either of the defendants found at the cottage?

DR GABRIEL: No.

DEFENCE: Thank you, that is all.

DR GABRIEL exits.

DEFENCE: Due to the unusual timing of Dr Gabriel's testimony I wonder if I might briefly delay calling Susan Ives to the stand?

JUDGE: That seems reasonable. Did you wish to adjourn?

DEFENCE: That won't be necessary, Your Honour. I can call Patrick Ives now if there are no objections.

JUDGE: Yes, please do.

DEFENCE: Call Patrick Ives.

PATRICK enters the witness box and takes the oath.

PATRICK: I swear by Almighty God that the evidence I shall give shall be the truth, the whole truth, and nothing but the truth.

DEFENCE: Mr. Ives, Can you tell us if anything unusual happened on the evening of 19th June last year?

PATRICK: No.

DEFENCE: Nothing at all?

PATRICK: No.

DEFENCE: Did your nanny, Kathleen Page, see you on the top floor of your property at around 8pm that evening?

PATRICK: Yes.

DEFENCE: When did you next see her?

PATRICK: Around fifteen minutes later.

DEFENCE: You heard her testimony earlier in this trial?

PATRICK: Yes.

DEFENCE: Would you agree with it?

PATRICK: In as far as it went.

DEFENCE: You mean there is more?

PATRICK: Much more.

DEFENCE: Please go on.

PATRICK: She became completely hysterical. Screaming and crying.

DEFENCE: Why was that?

PATRICK: Suzie had told she was no longer required and should leave on Monday. She begged me to intervene on her behalf.

DEFENCE: Did you?

PATRICK: No, I said I'd prefer Sunday.

DEFENCE: Why did your wife dismiss her?

PATRICK: She'd taken an afternoon off leaving the children with my mother. She was entitled to time off, of course, but we'd told her before that she had to give us proper notice.

DEFENCE: Why was Ms. Page so keen to keep her employment?

PATRICK: I suppose she enjoyed the job.

DEFENCE: Nothing else?

PATRICK: Nothing I know of.

DEFENCE: And you don't know why she took the afternoon off?

PATRICK: I think she said something about her mother, I can't remember.

DEFENCE: Was that the end of the conversation?

PATRICK: It was just the start.

DEFENCE: What else did you talk about?

PATRICK: It was just a lot more of the same. How she wanted me to get Suzie to change her mind about dismissing her.

DEFENCE: Did she mention removing a note from a book in the study?

PATRICK: No.

DEFENCE: Was Kathleen Page jealous of Lola?

PATRICK: Why would she be jealous?

DEFENCE: I was hoping you would tell us. Melanie Cooper has testified that you'd told her told her that there was no note inside the book in the study when you checked. Is that correct?

PATRICK: Yes.

DEFENCE: How many notes had been passed to you in this manner over the last couple of months?

PATRICK: About half a dozen.

DEFENCE: Do you know why Lola wanted to communicate with you in this way rather than calling you or sending an email?

PATRICK: I believe that she wanted there to be a paper trail, so to speak.

DEFENCE: What do you mean by that?

PATRICK: She involved Melanie so that someone else would know we were exchanging secret messages.

DEFENCE: Why would she do that?

PATRICK: As a safeguard, I suppose.

DEFENCE: I will come back to that. What did the notes say?

PATRICK: They were mostly suggestions to meet at the cottage.

DEFENCE: How many times did you meet?

PATRICK: Twice.

DEFENCE: Is that all? Twice?

PATRICK: Yes. Twice.

DEFENCE: What were the dates?

PATRICK: I couldn't tell you, exactly. Once towards the end of May and once about a week before the murder.

DEFENCE: If I might now turn to the knife which has been offered up as a potential murder weapon. Kathleen states that it belonged to you. Is that correct?

PATRICK: Yes.

DEFENCE: Do you have any idea where it was around 9.30pm on 19th June last year?

PATRICK: Yes. I was in my pocket.

DEFENCE: Why was it in your pocket?

PATRICK: I sketch using pencils. It is a hobby of mine. A knife is by far the most effective way of getting a decent point on a pencil.

DEFENCE: And you intended to sketch that evening?

PATRICK: I had used it to sharpen some pencils. I completely forgot it was in my pocket until Sunday morning when I put it back on my desk in the study.

DEFENCE: Mr. Ives, where were you at 9.30pm on 19th June?

PATRICK: I was at home.

DEFENCE: Doing what?

PATRICK: I really can't tell you, precisely. Possibly reading, possibly sketching, possibly watching TV.

DEFENCE: Are you aware that your mother has testified that you were out that evening? That is why it was Susan who took her a snack.

PATRICK: I'm afraid this is one of the very rare occasions that my mother is wrong. I was home all evening.

DEFENCE: Why didn't you go to play poker as arranged?

PATRICK: Circumstances made it impossible.

DEFENCE: Mr. Ives. You heard your mother's friend Laura Roberts testify that she heard your voice coming from Kathleen Page's room.

PATRICK: Yes, I heard that.

DEFENCE: Is she mistaken?

PATRICK: She is not mistaken.

DEFENCE: Which of you locked the door?

PATRICK: I cannot recall.

DEFENCE: You cannot recall?

PATRICK: That's what I said.

DEFENCE: It would have been fairly easy for anyone to leave the house that evening without being seen, would it not?

PATRICK: It would.

DEFENCE: How long would it take to walk to Orchard House Gatekeeper's Cottage?

PATRICK: Ten or fifteen minutes I would expect. There is a shortcut across the fields.

DEFENCE: The one that Kathleen used to take the children to the summerhouse?

PATRICK: Yes

DEFENCE: You knew about this path?

PATRICK: Yes. My mother told me that Kathleen had used it.

DEFENCE: Were you and Susan Ives happy?

PATRICK: Yes. Very happy. We still are.

DEFENCE: You expect us to believe that?

PATRICK: I don't expect anything, but it is true.

DEFENCE: Even though she knows that you were unfaithful.

PATRICK: I have never been unfaithful. I've told Suzie that I have never loved anyone else and that is true.

DEFENCE: Do you deny that you wrote the letters that were read out by the prosecution.

PATRICK: No. I wrote those letters.

DEFENCE: And where was your wife on the dates on the letters, May 22nd, and June 8th and 9th?

PATRICK: I have no idea.

DEFENCE: Was she away?

PATRICK: I've told you; I have no idea. I hadn't met her then.

DEFENCE: What?

PATRICK: The letters were written ten years ago. Before I met Suzie.

DEFENCE: Ten years ago! Then why did Lola have them in her bag when she went to meet you on June 19th?

PATRICK: She was selling them to me.

DEFENCE: Selling them. Blackmail, you mean?

PATRICK: That's an ugly word.

DEFENCE: How much did she want?

PATRICK: One hundred thousand pounds

DEFENCE: And you were going to pay it? One hundred thousand pounds for some old letters that you wrote before you had even met your wife!

PATRICK: The dates on the letters do not include the year and it is my handwriting. I knew that Lola would try to make Suzie think what the prosecution obviously thinks. That the letters had just been written.

DEFENCE: Couldn't you have just explained that wasn't the case? Are you admitting that she wouldn't have believed you?

PATRICK: I knew that she would believe me, but I didn't want her to see them anyway. I've always told Suzie that I've never loved anyone else so those letters might make her feel betrayed. I remember writing them as a result of a stupid childish infatuation but couldn't remember exactly what they said. Lola convinced me that they were very damaging.

DEFENCE: Can you afford one-hundred thousand pounds?

PATRICK: Of course not, but Lola told me that Stephen was making himself ill working so hard and barely making ends meet. She said they were going to sell up and make a fresh start somewhere. The money would help them do that and it would be good for me that they were gone.

DEFENCE: Where did the money come from?

PATRICK: I have various investments. I withdrew it in cash.

DEFENCE: Wouldn't a bank transfer have been easier?

PATRICK: Lola didn't want Stephen to know where the money had come from. She was going to put it into their account and then make up some story about an inheritance.

DEFENCE: She went to the cottage that night for you to hand it over.

PATRICK: Yes.

DEFENCE: But you didn't keep to the arrangement.

PATRICK: I wasn't aware that there was an arrangement.

DEFENCE: You didn't look to see if there was a note?

PATRICK: I did look, but there was no note.

DEFENCE: But if there had been you would have gone to the cottage.

PATRICK: Yes, I would have gone, given Lola the money, destroyed the letters and none of us would be stood here today.

DEFENCE: With the knife still in your pocket?

PATRICK: What does it matter? I didn't go to the cottage.

DEFENCE: Why did Lola involve Melanie in passing you the letters? Surely, if you are blackmailing someone, the fewer people who know the better. She couldn't know that Melanie wouldn't read them.

PATRICK: She might have wanted her to read them. She must have felt there was some danger in meeting me alone.

DEFENCE: Indeed. No further questions.

DEFENCE sits and PROSECUTION stands.

PROSECUTION: I'll ask you the one question that the defence didn't. Did you murder Lola Belamy?

PATRICK: No.

PROSECUTION: Thank you. No further questions.

DEFENCE: Call Susan Ives, please.

PATRICK exits and SUSAN enters the witness box and takes the oath.

SUSAN: I swear by Almighty God that the evidence I shall give shall be the truth, the whole truth, and nothing but the truth.

DEFENCE: Ms. Ives. What time did the conversation at the cricket club with Elliot Forrester take place?

SUSAN: Just after five.

DEFENCE: What did he tell you?

SUSAN: That Patrick was having an affair with Lola.

DEFENCE: Did you believe him?

SUSAN: Not at first but when he said he'd seen them together at the Gatekeeper's Cottage I became concerned.

DEFENCE: You then believed it?

SUSAN: Not entirely, but it worried me that it could be true.

DEFENCE: What happened next?

SUSAN: A group of us went back to the house. Patrick came home then, a little afterwards, Elliot left.

DEFENCE: Did you speak to him before he left?

SUSAN: Yes, I stopped him by the door and asked him not to repeat what he'd told me.

DEFENCE: Did you notice Melanie Cooper in the study?

SUSAN: No, I had my back to the study.

DEFENCE: Please go on.

SUSAN: Elliot left, and I was heading back to the living room when I heard Paul Harrison ask Patrick if he would be round later to play poker and Patrick reply that he'd try to make it but couldn't guarantee he'd be there. I knew that Patrick wouldn't know that I had overheard this conversation, so I asked him if he fancied coming with me to Lisa's. He then replied that he couldn't because he'd promised to go to Paul's to play poker. Then he said, "Excuse me for a minute" and left the room.

DEFENCE: Did you see where he went?

SUSAN: Yes. Our guests started to leave and, as I was showing them out, I saw him standing by his desk in the study.

DEFENCE: Did you see him take a book off the shelf?

SUSAN: No. You cannot see the bookshelf from the doorway.

DEFENCE: What happened next?

SUSAN: We had dinner then Margaret, Patrick's mother, went out into the rose garden, Laura went for a lie down and the children went up to their room. I went through into the living room with Patrick.

DEFENCE: How long were you in there?

SUSAN: Not long. Ten or fifteen minutes maybe. I kept thinking about what Patrick had been doing in the study before dinner so I eventually asked Patrick if he would say goodnight to the children for me.

DEFENCE: Was this the usual arrangement?

SUSAN: He liked to spend a little time with them after the nanny had put them to bed. He seemed to have forgotten that evening, so my comment was a reminder.

DEFENCE: I see. Go on.

SUSAN: When he went upstairs, I went into the study to see what he'd been doing at the desk. I found one of the drawers locked but there was nothing unusual in that and I knew where he kept the key. I opened the draw and found it stuffed with fifty-pound notes.

DEFENCE: Did you count them?

SUSAN: No, but I could see there was a lot. After what Elliot had said, I got it into my head that the money was so that he could run away with Lola somewhere and pay cash for everything so they couldn't immediately be traced.

DEFENCE: What did you do next?

SUSAN: I rang Stephen Bellamy. Shall I repeat what I said?

DEFENCE: Was your conversation as reported by Kathleen Page?

SUSAN: Word for word.

DEFENCE: Then you don't need to repeat. What did you do next?

SUSAN: I called up to Patrick that I was going to Lisa's, put my coat on and went out of the front door but went round the house toward the back gate.

DEFENCE: Did you have a plan of action?

SUSAN: Not really. I just knew that I had to speak to Stephen.

DEFENCE: Go on.

SUSAN: I looked up to the children's bedroom and noticed the window was open. I'm always telling the nanny to close the window when the children go to bed, but she doesn't take any notice. I ran back to the house to do it and, as I went up the stairs, I could hear Patrick talking and thought he must be in the children's bedroom but when I reached the top floor, I realised that he was in nanny's room. She was begging him to change my mind about dismissing her.

DEFENCE: OK. So, then you went to meet Stephen Bellamy.

SUSAN: I closed Kathleen's door and…

DEFENCE: You then went directly to the back gate.

SUSAN: I know what you are doing. I heard you questioning Patrick like he was the one that murdered Lola, but I must tell you everything. I locked Kathleen's bedroom door. I locked the pair of them in her room. That is why he wouldn't tell you who locked the door. It was me.

DEFENCE: Your Honour.

JUDGE: She's your witness. Ms. Ives, please confine yourself to answering the questions put to you.

DEFENCE: Thank you, Your Honour. Please tell us what happened when you met Stephen at the back gate.

SUSAN: It was just as Stephen said. We drove out to Astbury then put some petrol in at Congleton before returning to Chadwick. Everything was as he told you. After he'd called the hospitals, we went out and retraced Lola's steps and I said we might as well go there.

DEFENCE: Go where?

SUSAN: To the Gatekeeper's Cottage.

DEFENCE: You've never mentioned this before. It is not part of your statement to the police, nor have you ever mentioned it to me. Why are you telling us this now?

SUSAN: I want to tell you everything.

DEFENCE: Did you go to the cottage?

SUSAN: Yes.

DEFENCE: Your Honour, might I have a word with my client?

SUSAN: No. I want to carry on.

JUDGE: Your client appears to be reluctant.

DEFENCE: Susan, I must recommend…

SUSAN: You won't change my mind. I want to tell you everything that happened that night.

DEFENCE: But we've already had Mr. Bellamy's testimony. He said he drove you straight home.

SUSAN: Yes, and I will tell you why.

DEFENCE: Just a moment. Let us make sure we understand correctly. Was it your idea to go to the cottage?

SUSAN: I suppose it was a kind of joint decision. Stephen wondered if Lola might have gone to the cottage and become ill or had an accident, something like that, and I said we should go to check.

DEFENCE: What time was this?

SUSAN: About ten-fifteen.

DEFENCE: Was the cottage locked?

SUSAN: That's the thing. It was in complete darkness, and we assumed it would be locked, but when Stephen turned the door handle the door opened.

DEFENCE: And you went in?

SUSAN: Yes. Stephen was looking for a light switch. You would assume that it would be on the wall beside the door, but he couldn't find it, so he went back to the car to fetch a torch. As I was waiting, my eyes were getting accustomed to the dark, I went into the living room, and I thought I could make out the outline of a table lamp. As I reached for it, I tripped and fell, knocking the lamp to the floor.

DEFENCE: Did you see what you had tripped over?

SUSAN: I did when Stephen came in with the torch.

DEFENCE: What was it?

SUSAN: Lola. I was practically lying on top of her. (*She begins to sob.*)

DEFENCE: I would seriously recommend that we take a break.

SUSAN: I'd rather get it over with. Stephen helped me up and just stood looking at Lola for a while then he said, "Oh my darling, did they hurt you?" After a moment he said, "She's been murdered." Then I thought I heard someone moving outside and I screamed. I told Stephen that I thought I'd heard someone, but he said no one was there, but we should leave. I said, "We can't leave her" and he said, "There's nothing we can do for her." He started to lead me back outside and I said that we should call an ambulance, but he said it was too late, and we would be suspects if anyone knew we were there.

DEFENCE: Can you remember exactly what he said?

SUSAN: Yes, he said, "I'm sorry, Suzie but, even though this is nothing to do with us, it will look suspicious that we were here. Even though we are completely innocent, people will say we did this."

DEFENCE: He said this to you in the car?

SUSAN: No. we had just left the cottage and were standing in front of the car.

DEFENCE: What happened next?

SUSAN: Stephen took me home. He said that the police would ask questions, and we should both tell them everything that happened except leave out going to the cottage.

DEFENCE: What did you do when you got home?

SUSAN: I went into the kitchen to get a bag for my coat and noticed the fruit. I remembered that Patrick wouldn't have been able to take his mother a snack, so I took some up for her.

DEFENCE: Was the conversation with Mrs. Ives as she described?

SUSAN: Yes.

DEFENCE: Then, please go on.

SUSAN: I went up to the top floor and unlocked Kathleen Page's room. She was sat on the bed, her face like stone, Patrick was sat at the desk sketching. He stood up and as he passed me said, "I didn't know you had it in you," and I said "Neither did I." There is not much to say after that.

I went downstairs and flicked the porch light on and off as agreed with Stephen then went through to the sitting room. I didn't sleep, of course. We heard that Lola's body had been found at the cottage around lunchtime on Sunday and on Monday evening Stephen and I were both arrested.

DEFENCE: This is a full and entire account?

SUSAN: Yes.

DEFENCE: Why have you now decided to tell us that you went to the cottage having previously agreed with Mr. Bellamy to leave it out of your stories?

SUSAN: I don't want suspicion to fall on Patrick. Whoever murdered Lola, he had nothing to do with it. I have told you the truth, I locked him in the nanny's room, and he was still there after I had seen Lola's body with my own eyes.

DEFENCE: Thank you. No more questions.

DEFENCE sits and PROSECUTION stands.

PROSECUTION: Things have taken quite a turn, haven't they? Are you familiar with the back lane that leads from the bypass to the grounds of Orchard House?

SUSAN: Yes.

PROSECUTION: You wouldn't have any problem locating it?

SUSAN: No. I don't think so.

PROSECUTION: You are aware that this is a shorter route?

SUSAN: Yes.

PROSECUTION: You could easily reach Orchard House from Congleton in about fifteen minutes taking that route.

SUSAN: Yes.

PROSECUTION: Then, why didn't you take it?

SUSAN: Because we weren't going to the cottage. We didn't think about going there until later.

PROSECUTION: Why not? You knew Lola had gone there.

SUSAN: I didn't expect she'd still be there. As I have explained, Patrick couldn't have kept the appointment.

PROSECUTION: How did you get grease stains on your coat?

SUSAN: It wasn't grease; it was blood.

PROSECUTION: I'm glad that you had the common sense to correct your story. Whose blood was it?

SUSAN: Lola's, of course.

PROSECUTION: How did it get onto your coat?

SUSAN: As I explained I tripped and fell onto her. The blood was on her dress.

PROSECUTION: Oh yes, of course. Have you told us everything now, Ms. Ives?

SUSAN: Yes.

PROSECUTION: You are aware that you have contradicted your co-defendant's account of that evening.

SUSAN: He just left something out. I'm sure you can understand why.

PROSECUTION: What I understand is my business. Why have you now decided not to stick to the story that you agreed on?

SUSAN: I have already explained. I don't want anyone thinking Patrick could have been responsible.

PROSECUTION: Isn't it because you became concerned about the DNA evidence against you?

SUSAN: No.

PROSECUTION: You hastily concocted some fairy tale to explain why you had been at the cottage.

SUSAN: No.

PROSECUTION: The truth is that you didn't take the back lanes to Chadwick that night but took the direct route to Orchard House, confronted Lola Bellamy in the cottage and stabbed her to death.

SUSAN: No.

PROSECUTION: No further questions.

DEFENCE: Thank you, Susan. You may stand down.

SUSAN exits the witness box.

DEFENCE: Your Honour, in the light of Ms. Ives testimony I would like to re-question Stephen Bellamy, but before I do that, I need to advise you that a new witness has come forward with evidence vital to the trial. I would like permission to call him after Mr. Bellamy's re-examination.

JUDGE: This is a witness that has come forward after the submissions?

DEFENCE: He presented himself at this court a little while ago and I have only just become aware of his evidence. I think that the prosecution will agree that some aspects of this case remain unexplained. I believe this witness will help to fill in some of the gaps.

JUDGE: (*To PROSECUTION.*) Do you have any opposition?

PROSECUTION: It is a little irregular.

JUDGE: So is calling a prosecution witness whilst the defence is presenting its case.

DEFENCE: It is not without precedent, Your Honour.

JUDGE: I'm aware of that. I will allow it.

DEFENCE: Thank you, Your Honour. I will ask my assistant to prepare him to give evidence. Meanwhile can I have Stephen Bellamy back on the stand?

STEPHEN enters the witness box and takes the oath.

STEPHEN: I swear by Almighty God that the evidence I shall give shall be the truth, the whole truth, and nothing but the truth.

DEFENCE: Mr. Bellamy, did you hear Susan Ives's testimony?

STEPHEN: Yes.

DEFENCE: Would you agree with it?

STEPHEN: Yes.

DEFENCE: It is completely accurate?

STEPHEN: Yes, but there is something she doesn't know.

DEFENCE: What is that?

STEPHEN: I went back to the cottage after I took her home.

DEFENCE: For what purpose?

STEPHEN: I wanted to just be near Lola.

DEFENCE: So, you just went to sit with her.

STEPHEN: No. I took some antiseptic wipes and cleaned every surface that we had touched. I didn't know that Suzie had touched the lamp.

DEFENCE: Then you sat with your wife's body.

STEPHEN: No, I sat in the car.

DEFENCE: For how long?

STEPHEN: Until it started to get light.

DEFENCE: Did you remove anything from the cottage?

STEPHEN: No.

DEFENCE: Thank you, that is all.

DEFENCE sits and PROSECUTION stands.

PROSECUTION: So, we finally know why there were two sets of tyre prints outside the cottage that match your car. Have you told us everything?

STEPHEN: Yes.

PROSECUTION: You say that you didn't remove anything from the cottage.

STEPHEN: That is correct.

PROSECUTION: What about your wife?

STEPHEN: I don't know what you mean.

PROSECUTION: You removed her jewellery, didn't you?

STEPHEN: No. I didn't give a thought to her jewellery.

PROSECUTION: I think you did. I put it to you that after the pair of you had murdered your wife, you took Susan Ives home then went back to the cottage with the express purpose of making the scene look like a robbery gone wrong so that suspicion would fall on Darren York.

STEPHEN: No.

PROSECUTION: You were aware of his conviction.

STEPHEN: Yes, but...

PROSECUTION: Thank you. Finally, we are getting somewhere. No more questions.

DEFENCE: Thank you, Mr. Bellamy. I'd like to call the additional witness, Tom Williams.

STEPHEN exits, and TOM enters the witness box and takes the oath.

TOM: I do solemnly, sincerely and truly declare and affirm that the evidence I shall give shall be the truth, the whole truth, and nothing but the truth.

DEFENCE: Mr. Williams, where were you in the evening of June 19th last year.

TOM: Orchard House, well, the gardens, anyway.

DEFENCE: What were you doing there?

TOM: Trespassing, I suppose.

DEFENCE: I'll rephrase, why were you there?

TOM: I was planning to sleep in the summerhouse.

DEFENCE: Are you homeless?

TOM: No. I have a place in Wilmslow, but I don't stay there much.

DEFENCE: When you say that you have a place, you are referring to your parent's house.

TOM: My father's.

DEFENCE: You enjoy a lifestyle that involves moving around a lot, staying with friends or wild camping?

TOM: Or sleeping in a handy summerhouse, yes.

DEFENCE: How did you become aware of the summerhouse as a potential place to spend the night?

TOM: It was a month or so earlier. I'd hitched a lift back from a festival and been dropped off on the bypass. I walked down the lane that goes to Orchard House. There is a public footpath that goes right past the summerhouse and out onto the main road.

DEFENCE: Had you slept in the summerhouse before June 19th?

TOM: Once before, yes. It's nice, got chairs and a table, that sort of thing.

DEFENCE: What time did you arrive there on June 19th?

TOM: I got the 19.45 bus from Wilmslow so it would have been just around 8pm. The bus stop is right outside.

DEFENCE: What did you take with you?

TOM: Not much. I had my rucksack with my sleeping bag in it and a water bottle.

DEFENCE: You stayed in the summerhouse the whole time?

TOM: No. I decided I had better go for a pee before it got too dark because I'd forgotten to take a torch. I had my phone, but I didn't want to waste the battery.

DEFENCE: What time was this?

TOM: Nine-thirty.

DEFENCE: You are sure.

TOM: I checked the time on my phone to see how long it would be until it was completely dark.

DEFENCE: Go on.

TOM: I was standing in the bushes when I heard noises.

DEFENCE: What did you hear?

TOM: I heard a woman say, "Don't you dare touch me" then there was a scream.

DEFENCE: Where did the voices come from?

TOM: Sounded like they came from the cottage.

DEFENCE: Did you make any sound yourself?

TOM: Yeah, I was so taken by surprise I kind of grunted.

DEFENCE: Could you demonstrate?

TOM: I said "Uh." as in, "Uh. What's that?"

DEFENCE: Were you concerned by the scream?

TOM: Not really. I mean some girls scream all the time, don't they? I thought it was just someone messing about.

DEFENCE: Did you go to investigate?

TOM: I thought about it, but then I heard someone coming. I could hear the footsteps on the gravel path. I thought, "Whatever is going on in that cottage, I don't want to know" and went back to the summerhouse.

DEFENCE: What did you think it might be?

TOM: Someone dealing drugs, or taking drugs, maybe. I don't know.

DEFENCE: Did you then stay in the summerhouse?

TOM: For a bit, but then I heard a car.

DEFENCE: What time was this?

TOM: Quarter past, half past ten, something like that.

DEFENCE: What did you do?

TOM: Well, I thought if it had been some sort of drug deal going down earlier maybe someone might have called the police.

DEFENCE: Was it the police?

TOM: No. I packed up my rucksack and slipped round to the front of the cottage and saw it was just an ordinary hatchback.

DEFENCE: What did you do?

TOM: I sat in the bushes and watched them for a bit.

DEFENCE: You could see them quite clearly?

TOM: Yes, they left the engine running and the headlights on.

DEFENCE: Who did you see?

TOM: A man and a woman. They went into the cottage.

DEFENCE: Was it locked?

TOM: No. After a second, he came out again and went back to the car. I could see he'd gone to fetch a torch. He went back into the cottage and then I heard a scream.

DEFENCE: Then what?

TOM: They came out and he was trying to calm her down.

DEFENCE: Do you remember what he said?

TOM: Yes. I remember it exactly. He said, "I'm sorry, Suzie but, even though this is nothing to do with us, it will look suspicious that we were here. Even though we are completely innocent people will say we did this." Then they got in the car and left.

DEFENCE: Did you go into the cottage to see what they were referring to?

TOM: I did not. Whatever it was, I wanted nothing to do with it.

DEFENCE: Did you have any suspicions what it might have been?

TOM: I still thought it was something to do with drugs. Never occurred to me that it would be anything more serious.

DEFENCE: What did you do then?

TOM: I decided that it was best not for me to stay the night, so I started to go then I realised I'd dropped my water bottle. It clips onto my rucksack but it's not very secure. I spent a couple of minutes looking for it and then gave up.

DEFENCE: Where did you go?

TOM: I walked home. It took me a couple of hours.

DEFENCE: Why didn't you come forward with this information before today.

TOM: I didn't know anything about it. I tend not to follow the news much, too depressing. I got talking to someone at Glastonbury last weekend and he asked me where I was from. I said, "Wilmslow" and he said, "Near where that murder was" and I said, "What murder?" Then he showed me the story on his phone. I got back here as quick as I could.

DEFENCE: I'm grateful that you did, Mr. Williams. No further questions.

DEFENCE sits and PROSECUTION stands.

PROSECUTION: You say that you are of no fixed abode.

TOM: Something like that.

PROSECUTION: Do you have independent means?

TOM: What does that mean?

PROSECUTION: What do you do for money?

TOM: I get by.

PROSECUTION: How?

TOM: A bit of busking, sometimes.

PROSECUTION: Oh. Begging.

TOM: Busking. It's not the same thing.

PROSECUTION: Where do you do that?

TOM: Wilmslow, Macclesfield, Manchester, sometimes.

PROSECUTION: So much of your time is spent in the local area?

TOM: Yes.

PROSECUTION: Do you know anyone associated with this case.

TOM: I kind of know Daz. Darren.

PROSECUTION: Kind of?

TOM: Seen him around, that's all.

PROSECUTION: Did he contact you about this case at all?

TOM: No.

PROSECUTION: You are telling me that you only knew the details of this case a few days ago.

TOM: That is correct.

PROSECUTION: Even though you know one of the key witnesses and spend much of your in the local area.

TOM: Yes.

PROSECUTION: That is all.

DEFENCE: Thank you, Mr. Williams, you may step down.

TOM exits the witness box.

DEFENCE: I have no more witnesses, Your Honour.

JUDGE: Very well. Let us proceed with closing remarks.

PROSECUTION: Thank you, Your Honour. Ladies and Gentlemen of the jury, you have now heard the evidence of all the witnesses. You will have noticed that the two defendants have the same circle of friends, but very different lifestyles. Mr. Bellamy is struggling financially. He has debts; he cannot afford to keep up with his friends in his choice of car, he cannot even afford to have effective repairs made to his property. Patrick Ives has suggested that money is a prime contributor to the reasons behind the murder of Charlotte Bellamy and, perhaps, that is something we should consider.

Susan Ives is extremely rich. Not only can she afford a full-time nanny, she also employs staff to clean and cook for her. This is not necessary to support her career; no evidence has been provided to suggest that she has done a day's work in her life. Instead, she spends her day doing whatever she pleases, her wealth taking care of any domestic responsibilities. I'm not suggesting for a moment that it is her duty as a woman to attend to these responsibilities herself, of course not, but I do suggest that her lifestyle has bred in her a sense of entitlement, an arrogance, a belief that it is her absolute right to live such a privileged existence.

Divorce would be a disaster for Susan. Whatever settlement or maintenance payments were agreed, she would not be able to continue to live her carefree, easy life. Wealth on its own is not an evil thing but the effect it has had on Susan Ives is catastrophic.

But what of the facts of this case? Let us first deal with the matter of motive. I hold the view that no one, not a single soul, has a reasonable excuse for murder. Whether the circumstances involve cruelty, revenge, financial reward or the need to silence the victim, the taking of another person's life is abhorrent to almost all of us. But there are a few who have no empathy, no sense of what is right or wrong, a belief that the normal rules of morality do not apply them, and Susan Ives is one of those few.

This is a woman who was willing to break her father's heart by marrying the man that he begged her to stay away from. We will never know why Charles Thorne had such a loathing for Patrick Ives, but this is the first indication that Susan had little regard for the feelings of others. After her father died, Susan returned, triumphant, to Chadwick and wasted no time in showing off her victory over her father by buying a substantial property a stone's throw from the family home that soon began a descent into a crumbling white elephant: a blot on the beautiful landscape of Chadwick where Susan Ives reigned supreme.

But she was not a benevolent monarch. Poor Kathleen Page and Melanie Cooper dared to step out of line and were swiftly dealt with. Anyone who crossed Susan Ives soon felt her wrath and, sadly, Charlotte Bellamy suffered the ultimate consequence for threatening her regime.

She had the motive, and she also had the means and the opportunity. It was obvious from the very start that the story Stephen Bellamy and Susan Ives concocted of their complete ignorance of the fate that befell Lola in that cottage would never stand interrogation. However, Stephen stuck to it faithfully when he took the witness stand only for Susan to renege on the deal the moment she opened her mouth.

As it happens, I believe that her testimony to be substantially true. From the time when Elliot Forrester informed her of the affair, her every move was a revelation. She returned to her home full of rage which she hid under a smiling mask. She claims that she was unable to see the bookshelf in which Melanie Cooper places the book with the note from

Lola Bellamy, but I suggest that the mirror changes the angle of view making the bookshelf visible. It took her just a moment to retrieve that note and digest its contents. She later spied on her husband as he stood at his desk and then got him out of the way so that she could examine the contents of the drawer. She locked her husband in a room with the despised Kathleen Page to prevent him interfering with her plan, then proceeded to the cottage accompanied by Stephen Bellamy with a knife in her bag and murder in her heart. Patrick claims he had the knife produced in evidence in his pocket. It is up to you, the jury, to decide whether you believe that, but it is of little consequence. The knife used in this attack was a common type and Susan would have had access to several that could have done the job.

Her account of the drive to Astbury corroborates what Stephen told us, which is both incoherent and unconvincing, but her reasons for involving Stephen are clear. By making him an accomplice, he is not going to contradict any part of her account of the evening. I must make it clear that they do not have one shred of an alibi. Their claim that they took the longer, more time-consuming route back to Chadwick is laughable. The timings of the petrol purchase and the assumed time of the murder work perfectly. It is plausible that they took the bypass route to the cottage, committed the murder, then returned to the bypass and on to Chadwick where they were seen by Darren York. Not only did Darren York see them but Susan Ives saw him, possibly giving her the idea of constructing their prosperous alibi. Stephen Bellamy later returns to the cottage to remove any DNA evidence and make it look like a robbery. Whether this was his own idea or at Susan's insistence we don't know, but he made a fatal mistake in failing to wipe the lamp, meaning that they have had to change their stories at the very last moment.

I have chosen my words carefully when referring to the *assumed* time of the murder. The defence has already drawn attention to the fact that David Thorne did not see a car in the vicinity of the cottage. We have also heard from a member of what I will call the alternative society stating that he saw the defendants later than the assumed time for the murder. But let us remember who David Thorne is. He is Susan's devoted brother who has stated in this courtroom that he would do anything for her. However, it is of no consequence whether the murder took place at 9.30pm or after 10pm. The defendants do not have a reasonable alibi for either time. For this reason, the evidence you have heard from the rather dubious last-minute witness is irrelevant.

The only person with a motive to kill Charlotte Bellamy is Susan Ives. The fact that she drew Stephen Bellamy into her terrible plot is testament to the type of person she is. She had the motive, means and opportunity and Stephen did nothing to stop her. Ladies and gentlemen of the jury, you have heard the evidence. If you are satisfied that you are sure of their guilt, you must convict both Susan Ives and Stephen Bellamy of the murder of Charlotte Bellamy.

PROSECUTION sits and DEFENCE stands.

DEFENCE: Are you satisfied, ladies and gentlemen? Forgive me, but I fail to see how you can be. The prosecution has placed much emphasis on character. That Susan Ives is the sort of person that might commit a murder. But there is also the rather old-fashioned notion of evidence to be considered. Susan and Stephen spent the evening together, of that there is no doubt, but they have accounted for their whereabouts and are able to support this through sightings and the timing of an electronic card payment. But what of the evidence provided by the prosecution? Well, there was either a car in front of the cottage or there wasn't depending on which of the prosecution witnesses you believe. It is left to a defence witness to clarify that the car was there, but not at the time the prosecution would have liked.

Then we have an aggrieved employee with a grudge against Susan, eavesdropping on a private phone call. A sacked employee who tells us that she placed a note in a book that no one has been able to produce. A knife entered into evidence as the murder weapon which the prosecution now chooses to distance itself from claiming that it could be any similar knife.

The task before you is a simple one. Do you believe the account given to you by both Stephen Bellamy and Susan Ives to explain their whereabouts and their activities of that dreadful evening in June last year? They have both told you the same thing. Granted, Stephen initially failed to tell you part of the story, which is deeply regrettable, but do please consider that what he did tell you was entirely the truth. Susan volunteered information that did nothing to help their case and might have caused serious damage had we not been surprised by the appearance of Tom Williams who was able to verify the words spoken by Stephen when they came out of the cottage. Please remember that Susan did not know that Stephen's words had been overheard, but Tom Williams confirmed that they are exactly the words she repeated for us. Are they the words of someone who has just participated in a murder? I think not.

The prosecution has described Susan as an extremely wealthy woman who lives an idle life surrounded by servants who wait on her hand and foot, but the picture they have painted is wholly inaccurate. If you knocked on the door of the Ives house it would be Susan who answered. If she invited you in for a cup of tea, it would be Susan who made it for you. If you needed a lift back to Alderley Edge railway station it would be Susan who would drive you. She is not a member of some landed aristocracy. She is just an ordinary woman from a humble background who has a bit of help around the house with the cleaning and cooking and a nanny to help with the children.

The prosecution has spent considerably less time in describing Stephen Bellamy and with good reason. They would like you to believe that he is a weak and small minded man entirely under the spell of Susan Ives, a woman that, in reality, he barley knows. The truth is that Stephen is a hard-working individual who was utterly devoted to his wife and was doing everything he could to turn their fortunes round after the great misfortune of the firm in which he was a partner going under.

Susan Ives and Stephen Bellamy can never get back what they have lost. He has lost a wife whom he loved deeply. Whether she was deserving of that love depends on whether you believe Patrick Ives's story of blackmail or Elliot Forrester's story of infidelity. Perhaps you feel she was undeserving in either case. Susan has lost that happy confidence that her husband was always truthful with her. But at least they still have their freedom, and I ask you not to take that away.

It is my belief that Susan and Stephen are entirely innocent of the crime they are accused of but please remember that it is not my duty to prove that they are innocent. The prosecution must prove them guilty and that is something that they have failed to do. Thank you.

DEFENCE sits.

JUDGE: (*To the jury.*) That concludes the case for the defence, and it is now your duty to retire to consider your verdict. If you are not convinced that either or both of the defendants are guilty of the offence, then you must find them not guilty. However, if you are convinced, beyond reasonable doubt, that one or both of them did commit this crime then you must find them guilty. It is within your power to find one defendant guilty and the other not guilty. I will accept a majority verdict. Please follow the direction of the court usher.

USHER: Court rise.

END OF ACT TWO

ACT THREE

During the interval, the USHER assists the jury in discussing their verdict and reaching a decision. A FOREMAN is elected.

USHER: Court rise. (*All Rise and JUDGE enters.*)

JUDGE: (*To the jury.*) Will your foreman please stand. (*He/she does.*) Have you reached your verdict?

FOREMAN: We have.

JUDGE: In the case of Stephen Bellamy do you find the defendant guilty or not guilty?

FOREMAN: (*As decided by the jury.*)

JUDGE: Is that the verdict of you all or a majority?

FOREMAN: (*As decided by the jury.*)

JUDGE: In the case of Susan Ives do you find the defendant guilty or not guilty?

FOREMAN: (*As decided by the jury.*)

JUDGE: Is that the verdict of you all or a majority?

FOREMAN: (*As decided by the jury.*)

JUDGE: Thank you. You may sit down. (*The actor playing JUDGE takes off the wig and addresses the audience directly.*) Well, I expect you want to know if you got it right or not! Well, I can tell you that

If the jury found one defendant guilty, you were half right,
If the jury found the defendants not guilty, you were spot on,

If the jury found the defendants guilty, you've messed up, they were both not guilty.

I will let the actor who played the actual murderer explain why.

MARGARET: (*In actor's own voice.*) Thanks. (*The actor adopts the appearance of MARGARET. As MARGARET.*) Yes, it was me, Margaret. Patrick's mother. The clues were there all along. Who knew about the footpath between our house and Orchard House? Me, not Suzie. Who had a clear view through the window of what that cleaner was doing in the study? Me, not Suzie. Who could see exactly what it was that Patrick was putting in the desk draw? Me, not Suzie. Who, apart from the nanny, overheard Suzie's phone conversation? Who has absolutely no alibi between 8.30pm and just after 10pm? No one saw me during that time, well, apart from Charlotte.

You have heard a little about my background but let me add a bit more detail. Thirty odd years ago, shortly after Patrick was born, my husband left me for a younger woman. He just disappeared out of my life without a word. I didn't know where he had gone, and I never got a penny out of him. It was only after he died that I learned that he'd been living that whole time in Spain. Before he took off, we had been living in private rented accommodation and as soon as the landlord heard that he had an unemployed mother and baby in his flat, he turfed us out. I had to go to the council offices and beg them to find us emergency accommodation, otherwise we would have been sleeping on the street.

We eventually found ourselves in Chadwick and I managed to scratch a living doing various jobs. Patrick was an adorable child who accompanied me whenever he could and, when he was thirteen, took a job as a paperboy and handed over his meagre salary to help with the family budget. When I discovered that note concealed within a book in the study, I wondered if he might have acted differently if he knew how hard it was for a mother and child when they are deserted. Let me read the note to you. (*She takes out the note. Reading.*) "I'll be at the cottage around 9. Make any excuse you like, just be there. I've thought about what you said about Stephen, but he doesn't suspect anything, and the money will mean we can just take off whenever we want. I can't wait to be happy again and I know that you won't regret a thing. You always said that you wanted to make me happy."

I had suspected that there was something between Patrick and Lola for a while. About a month before the murder, she'd been at the house, and I saw them through the study window. He was looking down at something on his desk, but she was staring into his eyes like some lovesick puppy. I'd never liked her. Too much make-up and not enough personality. Then I heard her say, "Will you come?" and I heard him reply, "Yes. I'll be there." My world was shattered.

Of course, I completely misinterpreted that conversation and the note that I found on June 19th. I thought they were planning to go away together but what Patrick told you was true. That piece of dirt was blackmailing my son and was going to use the money to do a moonlight flit with her husband. If I had known that I wouldn't have done anything to prevent it.

You might wonder why I didn't just go to Patrick and Suzie and have it out with them. Tell them what I thought I knew and hope that Patrick would see sense. I can't answer that, but I acknowledge that wasn't thinking clearly. I wasn't a sensible middle-aged lady living a comfortable life, I was a young, abandoned mother walking to the council offices with my baby in arms convinced that I would have to sleep on the street. But please believe me when I say I didn't go to that cottage with the intention of murdering Charlotte Bellamy.

When I arrived, the front door was open. I closed it behind me and went through to the living room where she was stood with her back to me. She turned round and when she saw it was me said, "What the hell are you doing here?" I said, "I've come about Patrick" and she said, "What? He's hiding behind mummy?" I said, "He doesn't know I'm here; I found the note before he did. Please, Lola, you must stop this, no matter how much you love him." She said, "Love Patrick! I don't give a fuck about Patrick, but I'm going to take him for every penny I can get!" She came right up to me and said, "Now, fuck off before I do you some damage" and I said, "Don't you dare touch me" but she pushed me, and I fell backwards. I'm ashamed to say that pure rage took over. I took out the little gardening knife I had in my pocket and rushed at her, stabbing, stabbing, stabbing!

(*Pause.*) She screamed then fell to the floor. As I was staring at her I heard someone coming up the drive to the door. I thought I was about to get caught but then I heard something being posted through the letterbox and they went away again.

I looked down at the body and noticed jewellery and realised that I could make it look like a robbery by removing it. I went back to the house, washed the knife and went to bed. The following day, I buried the jewellery and the clothes I had been wearing in the rose garden. I don't know why I kept the note. Perhaps I thought I might need it.

I'm sorry that I murdered Charlotte Bellamy due to a stupid misunderstanding, but my biggest regret is doubting my son. If I'd had a little more faith, none of this would have happened. I've taken away one life and ruined three others. Stephen, Patrick and Suzie will spend the rest of their lives in a prison of my making. I won't ask for forgiveness; I will never forgive myself. (*She breaks down and starts to cry then the actor comes out of character. As herself.*) So, there you have it. Lola was murdered by a nice little old lady. Or was she an interfering old cow? I'll let you decide. Goodnight.

END

Printed and bound by CPI Group (UK) Ltd, Croydon, CR0 4YY

16/05/2025

01874082-0001